Best Wishes

A Whitlock

Also by Alan Whichello

Novels:
- Mushroom Cloud
- Kayak

Children's Books:
- The Hamsters' Great Escape
- Billy the Little Red Bus
- Percy the Reluctant Racing Pigeon

THE SCORPION TALES

EIGHT STORIES WITH A STING IN THE TAIL

Alan Whichello

Order this book online at www.trafford.com
or email orders@trafford.com

Most Trafford titles are also available at major online book retailers.

Printed in the United States of America.

ISBN: 978-1-4907-3150-6 (sc)
ISBN: 978-1-4907-3152-0 (hc)
ISBN: 978-1-4907-3151-3 (e)

Library of Congress Control Number: 2014905277

Trafford rev. 03/20/2014

www.trafford.com

North America & international
toll-free: 1 888 232 4444 (USA & Canada)
fax: 812 355 4082

Many thanks to Stuart Roper, whose advice and guidance through the early stages of my writing career have been tremendous. Without his support none of my books would have left the drawing board. His illustrations for my novels, especially my children's books, are a masterpiece.

I would also like to thank Stuart's wife, Fiona, whose editing skills are second to none. Her guidance has helped make my books a more exciting and enjoyable read.

And not forgetting my wife Gillian, for her support and patience in putting up with many disturbed nights when I got up early to spend hours in the office, writing down my ideas.

And, of course, thanks to Trafford, my publishers, for all their help.

Author's Note

Most of these stories are based on actual events and there is some truth in all of them, although I may have exaggerated and twisted the story to make it a more exciting and enjoyable read. Many readers will recognize some of the place names and locations, as I try to make the stories as true and realistic as possible. I hope you all have a good read, and not have too many nightmares.

Contents

THE PAIR OF BROGUES

CHAPTER 1

Ever since he started school at the age of five, Toby McGuire had been bullied. Maybe it was because he was the smallest in his class. Or maybe it was because of his curly mop of ginger hair.

"The other kids are just jealous of your curls," his mother always said as she was combing it before he went to school, but that didn't seem a very good explanation to Toby. "But why are they always picking on me?" he asked.

"Don't worry Toby" his mum replied. "They will soon grow out of it, and pick on somebody else."

But they didn't. It happened all through secondary school. Toby couldn't wait to leave school and get away from the torment. He started work at the local supermarket, and all was fine for the first week, then the bullying started all over again. It didn't help matters when he was checked over at the opticians and found to be short sighted, so had to wear glasses. But Toby ignored all his tormentors, and when he turned twenty he met a local girl down at the bakery. After a quick romance, Toby thought he had found a perfect partner and married her. They rented a small flat and for the first year Toby was very happy. At least he could come home and relax away from his tormentors.

But things soon changed. His wife, Jenny, started to put on weight, probably because she was a lousy cook and found it easier to buy a takeaway, so most evenings Toby and Jenny would have a McDonalds, or a pizza, and fish and chips on others. And that was the main cause of the arguments. No matter how much Toby ate, he never gained any weight. After the second year of marriage, Jenny weighed nearly twice as much as Toby who still had a slim nine stone figure. Very soon Toby was coming home to even more bickering and arguments.

He was sick of it all, the trouble was he hated confrontation and arguments and never spoke up for himself. Then one night after a bitter argument, Jenny lashed out and struck Toby across the face, maybe out of frustration, or maybe because he just didn't answer back. From then on Toby would often go into work with bruises or a black eye caused by Jenny's temper. This period in his life was when Toby was the most depressed.

One fine Saturday afternoon Toby was out down the town by himself. He liked to browse around the shops, especially charity shops, just to cheer himself up. It was amazing the good and sometimes new things that people would give to charity. Toby himself had donated and bought a few things, although his wife usually threw them away when she found them, or took them back to the charity shop to see if she could get the money back,

"I don't know why you buy this rubbish, you know we can't afford it!" she used to say.

But on this particular afternoon Toby found himself in the Red Cross Charity Shop on Broadstreet. This shop always had a lot of good quality clothes, and Toby wanted a new pair of trousers. He flicked through the coat hangers and found a nice pair, a bit old fashioned maybe but in nearly new condition.

"Can I try them on?" he asked the pretty shop assistant.

"Yes, certainly sir" she replied. "The cubicle's over there." She pointed to a small curtained area in the corner. Toby tried them on and was pleased with the way they fitted.

"I'll take them" he said as he emerged from the cubicle. "How much are they?"

The pretty shop assistant looked at the inside tab. "That will be eight pounds, sir" she said, smiling.

Toby paid the money and was just about to walk out when he spotted the shoe rack. He looked down at his own worn shoes and decided to have a look for a new pair. One pair stood out from the rest. They were brown leather, highly polished with raised stitching around the crown of the shoe.

They had an unusual white decorative top that was quite distinctive. Toby picked them up and looked at them more closely. The initials PS were written inside both shoes in red biro. He suddenly had an overwhelming urge to try on the shoes He slipped them on and tied the shoe laces. They fitted perfectly and looked brand new. He walked up and down the shop floor. The shoes seemed to be generating new life into his tired body. He then walked up to the counter.

"I will take these as well" he told the pretty shop assistant who had been watching him with great amusement.

"Ah, the pair of brogues" she said. "You don't see many of these around anymore. Do you want them wrapped, sir?" she asked "Can I keep them on?" said Toby. "They are so comfortable."

"Very well" said the pretty shop assistant. "That will be ten pounds." Toby felt around in his pocket and pulled out a five pound note and some loose change.

"I only have nine pounds fifty" said Toby. "Could I come in and pay you the rest tomorrow?

"We are not going to argue over fifty pence" replied the pretty shop assistant. "You've already bought some trousers, so you can take the shoes." Toby handed over the money and left the shop a happy man. He walked around the town for a little longer then decided to go home.

He had not felt this good for a long time; his depression had lifted and he felt alive. As soon as he opened the front door his wife shouted from the kitchen.

"Where have you been? I hope you haven't spent all your money, I want some to go down the bingo hall tonight." Toby felt in his pocket again, he hadn't got a penny left. He took off his shoes tiptoed up stairs and hid them under the wardrobe. Depression immediately came back, what was he going to tell his wife? Toby went downstairs and into the kitchen holding the pair of trousers over his arm.

"I bought these down at the charity shop" he said "There're nearly new and only cost eight pounds." He held up the pair of trousers to show his wife.

"What in hell do you want those old fashioned trousers for?" she screamed. "What's wrong with the ones you are wearing?" Toby didn't reply but just stood there. His wife held out her hand.

"Where's my money?" she said threateningly.

Toby sheepishly replied "I haven't got any left." Before he could get out of the way a fist punched him in the stomach. Toby fell to his knees gasping for breath.

"First thing tomorrow" his wife screamed, "You can take those trousers back to the shop and get your money back." She bent down to Toby's face and said "Do you understand?"

Toby grimaced and said "Yes, dear." The next day Toby got dressed, put on his new pair of brogues and slipped out without waking his wife. He was a bit early but he thought he would walk around until the shop opened, anything was better than staying at home. But the more Toby walked about in the brogues, the more confident he felt. He liked the pair of trousers. Why should he have to embarrass himself and ask for the money back? No, I am going to keep them he thought.

He was walking along the high-street when a man brushed past his shoulder. "Hey! Watch where you're going you clumsy idiot!" he heard himself say.

The man turned sharply and Toby recognized him immediately. It was Andy Butcher, one of the gang that used to bully him at school. He braced himself for an onslaught, but the man didn't seem to recognize him.

"I am very sorry sir" the man said. "I do apologize."

"Well, that's all right then" said Toby. "Just keep your eyes open next time". He couldn't believe what he had just said. For the first time in his life he had felt confident enough to confront somebody and actually answer them back. But his confidence was beginning to disappear on the way back home. He hadn't taken the pair of trousers back, what excuse could he give his wife? Then he thought to himself, why should I have to make an excuse? I will tell her the truth, if she doesn't like it, too bad.

Toby opened the front door and marched into the kitchen without taking his shoes off. His wife was busy heating up the pizza in the microwave; she picked up a rolling pin, and asked menacingly "Where's my money?"

Toby stood his ground. "I haven't got your money, because I am going to keep the trousers, along with my new shoes." He pulled up his trousers a little and flashed the new pair of brogues. His wife's face turned a bright red and she rushed at Toby with the rolling pin above her head. Toby didn't move, and then, just as she was about to bring it crashing down on his head his hand shot up and grabbed the rolling pin. With his other hand he shoved her backwards. She stood there for a few minutes gathering her thoughts. This shouldn't be happening, Toby had never stood up to her before; he must be drunk. She lunged at him again but this time Toby moved sideways at the last minute and his wife fell headlong against the corner of the kitchen table. She lay on the floor blood dripping down the side of her face from the gash on her forehead. Jenny began to cry and for the first time Toby felt sorry for her. He held out his hand and she grasped it. He then pulled her to her feet. It felt so easy, even though she weighed twice as much as him. She sat down on a chair holding her head. Toby picked up a tea towel, soaked it under the tap then went over to his wife. He held the towel over the cut on her forehead.

"Things are going to change around here" he said in a demanding voice. "You are going to start cooking wholesome meals. I don't want that slop you keep giving me night after night. Do you understand?" She didn't understand why her meek husband had suddenly changed, and was now ordering her around. But she nodded just the same.

"And another thing" he continued, "You will start washing my clothes, not just your own. Agreed?" Jenny agreed; her head was throbbing so badly she would agree to anything as long as she could have a lie down.

So from then on things started to improve for Toby, but only when he was wearing the brogues. He found out that as soon as he slipped out of the brogues, he became less confident and depressed so he only took them off last thing at night just before getting into bed. He even wore the shoes to work. If anybody started to ridicule him, then he became more aggressive and threatening. Toby was a changed man. He was no longer the wimp that everybody could bully and order around.

He started to go out drinking, leaving his wife at home working. He felt stronger, fitter and more able to take care of himself. His confidence grew more and more as long as he was wearing the brogues. But his wife was beginning to hate him, he was becoming more and more aggressive, she preferred him the way he was before: somebody she could control and manipulate.

Why had he changed? Why was he becoming more aggressive? His wife was determined to find out.

CHAPTER 2

Toby was enjoying his newfound freedom. For the first time in his life he didn't feel afraid of anybody or anything. He was, however, spending a lot of money down at the local pub. It was there that he met Trevor, a tall slim man, who was sitting alone at the bar. They started talking, Toby bought him a pint and Trevor returned the favour. After a few more drinks the conversation became more personal. Trevor remarked about the unusual smart shoes Toby was wearing and asked where he got them. Toby was now a bit intoxicated and nearly let slip his secret about the brogues, but managed to change the subject.

He noticed Trevor looking at his wallet when he bought him another drink, which unnerved him a bit. He decided to leave. He had told Trevor, if that was his real name, far too much about himself. And he was feeling a little worse for wear. He got up and said goodbye to Trevor then made his way to the toilets. When he had freshened up he popped back into the pub, but there was no sign of Trevor. He buttoned up his coat as he stepped outside. It was quite dark, but there was a full moon.

Toby started walking home and took the usual short cut down Peacocks Lane, a narrow alleyway between some shops. He was halfway along the alleyway when a man suddenly stepped out of a darkened doorway. The man grabbed Toby from behind and then he felt a sharp object sticking into his back.

"Give me your wallet or I'll knife you!" the stranger growled. Toby didn't think twice. Quick as a flash he swung around and grabbed the hand that was holding the knife. He then brought it down across his knee, knocking the knife free. The knife fell to the ground, but Toby was the first to pick it up. He swung around and stabbed the man in the stomach. It felt good as the knife sunk deep into the man's flesh. The man fell to his knees. Toby pulled out the knife and stabbed the man again and again. In all Toby stabbed him six times until he realized he was dead. He knelt down and wiped his blood-soaked hands on the man's jacket. Toby peered into the dead man's face and recognized him immediately. It was Trevor, the man who had befriended him in the pub not ten minutes ago. Toby slipped the flick knife into his own pocket and disappeared down the alley.

The body was discovered by a man walking his dog just an hour later. The story was broadcast on the early morning news. The police were looking for a slim man dressed in a three quarter length coat. The strange thing was, Toby thought while watching the news, nobody had mentioned his ginger hair, so perhaps he had got away with it? Anyway it was self-defence, so he did not feel guilty.

Toby never confessed to the police, mainly because he had enjoyed killing the man. He couldn't get it out of his mind, the knife sinking into the man's flesh. He began to stalk the streets at night, visiting pubs on the other side of town. It was in the Crown on Hazel Street that he bumped into Mark Rusher, the leader of the school gang. At first Mark didn't recognize him, until Toby introduced himself.

"Ah, it's the ginger geek from school!" Mark chuckled. "God, you haven't grown much, have you been on a diet?" he laughed out loud, much to the amusement of the other drinkers. Toby could feel his body becoming taut; he wanted to smash Mark's smug face. But he kept his anger under control.

"Can I buy you a drink, Mark?" He paused and added quietly "It will probably be your last."

"Well, if you're leaving, Ginger, I'll have a double whisky" replied Mark. Toby paid for the drink, and then made his excuse to leave. He waited outside on the opposite side of the road in a telephone box, where he had a perfect view of the front door of the pub. Twenty minutes later Mark emerged from the pub. Toby could see he wasn't very steady on his feet. He started walking up the street, so Toby followed, keeping his distance so as not to be heard. He guessed he lived nearby or else he would have driven or come with somebody else. Mark walked down Hazel Street for about half a mile then turned off into a dimly lit alleyway. Toby quickened his pace, now was his chance and probably his only change. He caught up with Mark, and then felt in his pocket for the flick knife.

"Hello again," he said as Mark turned around. "This is for all the torment you caused me at school" Before Mark could reply Toby had plunged the knife into his side. Toby felt the blade hit the ribcage and veer off, so he pulled the knife out and stabbed Mark in the heart. Mark died instantly without making a sound. But Toby didn't stop the stabbing; it was as though he was in a trance.

It was only when he heard footsteps behind him that he stopped. He dragged the body behind some bushes and hid until the person had passed. He cleaned up his bloody hands then piled leaves over the body. He made sure the coast was clear then disappeared into the night.

He knew it was only a matter of time before he was caught. But he felt justice had been done. Mark deserved to be killed he was a nasty piece of work that needed to be erased; he didn't have any remorse about what he had done. In fact he felt better than ever.

CHAPTER 3

Jenny had been watching her husband closely over the past weeks trying to work out why he had changed so much. She searched the pockets in his shirts, his trousers and his coats thinking he must be taking some sort of enhancing drug. But she found nothing.

She wondered if it could be all the drinking, but his behaviour had changed before he had started drinking and he didn't smoke. It was only when she noticed that the last thing he took off before he went to bed was his shoes and socks and then he would neatly tuck them under the bed out of sight. The more she thought about it, the more sense it made. He only ever wore the brogues. He polished them every morning without fail and they still looked as good as new. But how was she going to get rid of them? He would know they were missing as soon as he woke up.

Her chance came a few weeks later. Toby had woken up with a terrible headache.

"I'm not going into work today" he said to his wife. "I feel terrible." His wife replied "You stay in bed and I'll fix you a nice hot Lemsip. That will make you feel better."

She went into the kitchen and boiled the kettle. After she had made the hot drink, she dissolved six sleeping tablets in the cup and took the mixture up to her husband. He did look terrible, but she didn't really care. Jenny just wanted her old husband back. Toby eagerly drank the liquid and was soon sound asleep. Jenny crept into his room and pulled out the shoes. She crept downstairs and into the kitchen.

After examining them she had found nothing out of the ordinary, apart from a faded PS penned into the inside back of the shoe, which she presumed were the previous owner's initials. So she wrapped the shoes in some newspaper, put on her coat and hurried down to the charity shop. She was a bit breathless when she stumbled into the shop.

"Can I sell you these?" she said, holding out the brown and white brogues. "Look, they are brand new." The pretty shop assistant recognized them immediately.

"We sold a pair like this a couple of months ago" she said "but I can't give you any money for them, this is a charity shop."

"Very well," said Jenny not wanting to make a fool of herself. "Take them anyway, I think they're hideous." She left the shoes on the counter and hurried out of the shop. When she arrived home half an hour later Toby was still sound asleep

Jenny was getting a little worried when Toby had still not woken at five o'clock in the evening. I hope I haven't given him too many pills and he has gone into a coma, she thought. But one hour later Toby woke up. He still felt a little groggy, but very hungry. He shouted down the stairs.

"Can you bring me up a cup of tea and something to eat dear? I'm starving." A few minutes later his wife came into the room, she was carrying a bowlful of soup, some toast and a big mug of tea. Toby ate the soup and toast and quickly drank the tea.

"I feel a little better now" said Toby. "I think I'll get up and go out for a walk." His wife was horrified.

"No Toby, you stay in bed" she said. "You still don't look very well."

But Toby knew as soon as he put on the brogues he would feel a lot better. He sat up and felt under the bed, then slid on to the carpet and looked under the bed.

"Where are my shoes?" he shouted.

"I took them back to the shop" his wife replied. "I didn't think you wanted them anymore."

"You fool, woman!" said Toby "What did you do that for?"

Jenny didn't reply, she just stood there watching him. Toby got dressed, but already he didn't feel at all well.

"Not so strong now are we?" his wife mocked. "Not without those damn shoes." He looked at her menacing face and knew she had discovered his little secret.

CHAPTER 4

That evening Toby's wife was in heaven. She sat in front of the television, flicking between channels. Toby had made her supper, with a nice cup of chocolate and brought her two Mars bars. She was watching the History Channel. The programme was about serial killers.

Then suddenly she froze with fear. There staring at her on screen was a good looking bearded man. But it wasn't the man she was looking at, it was his shoes. They were the same brogues her husband had worn; there was no mistaking the brown leather, the bold stitching and the white decorative top. The man's name was Peter Sutcliffe, better known as the Yorkshire Ripper. She suddenly remembered the initials penned into the shoes: P S-Peter Sutcliffe. It had to be. A cold chill ran through her. Her husband had been wearing Peter Sutcliffe's shoes, the notorious killer that had stabbed and killed at least a dozen women. Jenny slowly began to control her fears, she had got rid of the shoes, and everything was as before. Her dear husband had returned to being a wimp. The wimp that she could order about all she wanted and if he objected, she lashed out and hit him.

The next morning, before his wife had woken up, Toby got dressed, put on his old pair of shoes and ran down the High Street to the Charity Shop. Toby had only one thing on his mind. He must get back the pair of brogues at any cost. He arrived ten minutes too early, the shop hadn't opened. He waited what seemed like an eternity. Then he spotted the pretty shop assistant walking toward him.

"Good morning sir" she said "Do you wish to buy something?"

"I sure do" replied Toby.

She unlocked the door and said "Come on in and look around." Toby made straight for the shoe rack. But his shoes were not there. He turned to the pretty shop assistant and asked "Did a woman bring in a pair of shoes yesterday; they were brown leather with bold stitching and a white fancy top?"

"Ah, you mean the brogues, sir" she said confidently. "I am sorry but we sold them to a man, soon after the woman brought them into the shop."

"Do you know the man's name and address?" asked Toby desperately, hoping he might be able to contact the man and offer him a good price for the shoes.

"I'm sorry sir" replied the shop assistant. "We don't take any of the purchaser's details." Toby fell to his knees and began to sob.

"I am sorry sir, were they very special?" she asked, concerned.

"Yes, very special" sobbed Toby as he picked himself up.

"We have some other shoes you could try on" she said feeling a bit guilty.

"That won't be necessary" replied Toby as he trudged out into the street. Toby was at rock bottom again, he had not felt this depressed for a long time. For the next two weeks Toby tried to stand up to his wife, but the fire in him had all but dwindled out. It wasn't long before his mocking workmates noticed the bruises and occasional black eye.

"Has your wife been giving you a right pasting again?" one of them said. The others thought this hilarious and bust out laughing. Toby just ignored them and retreated back into his own little world, a broken man.

On the rare occasion Jenny let Toby go for a drink down at the local pub, she always gave him enough money for just two pints. "I don't want you coming home drunk like you used to" she would say, followed by "Don't you stay out too late." Toby cheered up a bit when he had a couple of pints in him, especially if somebody else had bought him a drink.

On his way home one night he thought somebody was following him; he kept glancing behind, but could see nothing. But he could still hear footsteps and they seemed to be getting nearer. Toby quickened his pace and then sidestepped down a little alleyway.

He went a little further and stopped and listened. Everything was quiet and then he suddenly realized where he was. The dimly lit alleyway, the overgrown bushes along one side: it was where he had murdered Mark Rusher.

Then Toby felt a sharp pain in his back. He put his hand behind him and felt a knife, but before he could do anything the knife was withdrawn and he was stabbed again. Toby fell to his knees, and then he was stabbed again in the neck. He fell to the floor, blood gushing out of his wounds. He felt hands feeling inside his pockets and then pulling out his wallet. He managed to turn his head and looked straight at a brown leather shoe with bold stitching around the side and a decorative white top. Toby took a last gasp of air and then stopped breathing.

The murderer was never caught. So, if you happen to meet a stranger wearing brown leather brogues with bold stitching and a decorative white top, just make an excuse and walk away.

THE BOY WHO NEVER WAS

CHAPTER 1

I first met Kevin Peters at Blackstone Secondary School many years ago. I had just turned 11 years old, and Kevin was allocated to my class, 1B. After the teacher had introduced herself, we all had to stand up and tell the other pupils our names. I thought then that there was something strange about Kevin, but I couldn't quite put my finger on it. He stood awkwardly, as though he wasn't at ease with his stature. He was rather small for his age and quietly spoken, in fact the teacher asked him to speak up, much to the amusement of the others.

For the first 6 months nothing really happened. I became friends with two other boys, one I knew previously from primary school. But Kevin never really made any friends. I spoke to him occasionally, but he seemed very distant and didn't want to prolong the conversation. Academically Kevin was of above average intelligence. His best subjects were science and maths and in those he would always come top of the class. This was probably the cause of all his troubles and he became known as 'the geek' by the bigger boys. Kevin hated any form of physical activity, especially football or rugby, and would always try and make an excuse not to join in, saying he felt ill. He even brought in a note from the doctor saying he was allergic to water on his skin to avoid taking a shower with the rest of the boys. But on this particular day all the excuses didn't work. Mr Brady our PE instructor was adamant.

"Kevin you have given me enough excuses, there's nothing physically wrong with you. It will do you good and develop some muscles in your legs." It was the first rugby match that Kevin had participated in and he was the last boy to get picked. He was on the opposite team to me. Mark Rusher, a large muscley boy with a big ego and a big mouth was their captain. Most of the 1st year pupils were scared of him and did exactly what Mark told them to do, except for Kevin. He didn't like running or getting tackled, so when the ball was passed to him he froze. He stood there not knowing what to do.

"Run, run you stupid bastard!" I heard Mark Rusher screaming at the top of his voice. He was about to run, when a huge boy butted him in the shoulder at full speed. Kevin was sent sprawling into the air and landed a good ten feet away. He seemed to bounce a couple of times and then lay still in a crumpled heap. Mr Brady the PE Teacher came running over and I followed.

"Are you all right son?" asked Mister Brady. Kevin stretched himself out then stood up.

"Yes, Sir," he said with hardly a missed breath, "I am perfectly alright." I was standing less than 3 feet away and could see there was not a mark on him. It looked as though he had just walked on to the pitch. Most of the other boys had gathered around to get a closer look hoping to see a bit of blood or maybe a broken arm.

"Come along then" said Mr Brady, "the show's over. Let's get on with the game." Everybody took up their positions, except me. I couldn't take my eyes off Kevin. How could a boy of his size and stature be rugby tackled by a boy twice his size and not be injured?

"Come on you two!" Mr Brady's shout brought me back to reality. The game went on for another twenty minutes; fortunately Kevin did not get another touch of the ball. But Mark Rusher's team lost for the first time ever. As we made our way back to the changing room Mark was furious, he brushed passed me and came up behind Kevin.

"You had better watch your back, geek" he snarled, "you cost us the match!"

For the next four weeks Kevin kept a low profile, keeping well away from Mark Rusher and his gang. I took this opportunity to try and make friends with Kevin as he had no one else to talk to. But it was all one-sided although I did manage to find out where he lived, which it turned out was not far from my house.

"Would you like to come over to my house this Saturday" I blurted out. "I can show you my new computer."

"I don't think that's a good idea" said Kevin. "Thanks for the offer, but perhaps I had better leave it a few weeks until I have made my peace with Mark Rusher." I didn't have time to reply before he got on his bike and was gone.

It was inevitable that Mark and his gang caught up with Kevin and I witnessed the whole thing. It was at the end of the day. Most of the pupils had left the school, apart from a few stragglers, me included. As Kevin went to get his bike, Mark and his gang of about 5 boys were waiting for him behind the bike shed.

"Aha here's the little turd!" I heard Mark say. "I think you owe us some money as compensation for the game you cost us."

"But I don't have any money," said Kevin.

"Well then," snarled Mark, "then I think you deserve a good kicking." He pushed Kevin backwards and he fell to the ground. Before I could intervene, the boys had surrounded him and began kicking him. It was a couple of minutes before I managed to persuade Mark that Kevin had had enough and stop the onslaught.

They ran off laughing, leaving a pitiful Kevin whimpering in a huddled ball. I bent down to help him up. The whimpering suddenly stopped.

"Have they gone yet?" Kevin whispered to me.

"Yes," I replied. Kevin stood up without any help and brushed himself down.

"I must get home, I am late already. Thanks for your support Alan, but you must not put yourself in danger because of me. I am perfectly capable of looking after myself."

"But aren't you winded or bruised?" I asked, rather surprised after the severe kicking I had just witnessed.

"I'm fine" said Kevin, rather annoyed. "Don't worry about me!" as he got on his bike and cycled off down the road. I stood there for a few minutes thinking about what had just happened before making my way home.

For the next year nothing extraordinary happened. Kevin had been upgraded to class 3A, two classes above mine. I didn't see him much that year, only in the school playground at lunchtime. He was easy to spot standing all alone in a corner, usually reading a book. He still got bullied by Mark and his gang, but he never complained.

One day I asked him "Can I come around to your place this Saturday, and meet your Mum and Dad?"

"Mum and Dad are away for a week" he quickly replied.

"Haven't you any brothers or sisters?"

"No" he said, rather abruptly.

"Well then, who is looking after you?" I said.

"For God's sake, I am nearly forty!" he paused, "that is, fourteen years old. I can take care of myself."

My questions seemed to have made him nervous, but then he turned around and carried on reading, completely ignoring me. From then on our conversations became less frequent.

At the end of that year the school held an Open Day. All the pupils brought along their parents for the teachers to meet and show off what they had achieved during that year. My parents were rather disappointed at my achievements, but were amazed in the science lab when they saw the blackboard covered in problems such as: if pi x r = q what is the gas density required to support a man's weight of 74 kilos?

"Is that the sort of things you have to work out?" my Dad asked.

"No" I replied "that's Kevin working things out, he's brilliant at that sort of thing." I glanced around and saw him pouring liquids into a sample glass at the end of the classroom.

"Come on, I'll introduce you to him" I said, dragging my mother by the arm over to the bench

"Hello Kevin, this is my mother."

"Pleased to meet you Mrs Collins" said Kevin, rather nervously.

"Are your parents here?" asked my mother looking around the room.

"No I am afraid not" replied Kevin "they had to leave unexpectedly."

"Ask him over for tea this Saturday," I whispered in my mother's ear.

"Kevin, would you like to come over on Saturday? I am sure Alan would be glad of the company and we could have a barbeque in the garden if the weather is nice." Kevin hesitated then replied.

"That would be nice, thank you. Excuse me, I don't mean to be rude but I must get on with this experiment." He turned his back and carried on with his work.

"He seems a very strange boy!" Mum whispered to me when we were out of earshot.

"Yes" I replied "he is just a bit nervous and shy." As we were leaving I spoke to the Prefect who had been on the entrance door all evening greeting the parents.

"Did you meet Kevin's parents?" I asked.

"No, he came on his own" the Prefect replied. I thought this a bit strange but kept it to myself.

Saturday arrived and by 6 o' clock there was still no sign of Kevin. So I rode over to his house to look for him. I knocked on the front door and waited. I could see Kevin's bike chained to the porch post and there was no car on the driveway, so I presumed he would be in. I glanced up at the bedroom window and saw the curtains move, a few minutes later the door opened slightly and Kevin peered around the door.

"Are you coming over for tea? We are all waiting for you" I said softly. I didn't want to sound as if it was an order.

"Yes, just let me finish a few things and I'll join you." He closed the door and I heard him running upstairs. A few minutes later the door opened and Kevin stood there in his school uniform. I thought it a bit odd that he wasn't wearing anything casual, but didn't want to delay him any longer. We got on our bikes and rode home.

The evening tea was not a great success. Kevin picked at his food as though he was eating something foreign; he ate most of the salad but left the meat. He only drank water and did not have any desserts, and as for conversation Kevin only spoke when asked a question and then it was only to say yes or no.

After an hour Kevin made an excuse to leave, thanked my mother for the meal and left hurriedly.

"What a strange boy," was the first thing mum said when he had gone. "You do make some odd friends, Alan!"

CHAPTER 2

The school year was nearly over when the next incident happened; in fact it was the last day of school and everybody was looking forward to Christmas. And it was Mark Rusher who was the main culprit. He just wouldn't let things settle. And it was poor old Kevin that was the victim. Mark and his gang had lured Kevin up on to the flat roof above the gym. This was a favourite place for smoking and occasional drug taking. You entered through a trap door in the storage room. Nobody went up there, except the maintenance staff to service the large air conditioning units and water storage tanks, so it was a good hiding place for an occasional puff.

Why Kevin was fooled into going I just don't know, but as I was making my way to the bike shed something caught my eye on the roof. It was Kevin. I shouted, but he didn't hear me. The next minute he stepped back and slipped off the roof. I looked on in horror as his body hit the concrete path and he lay still. I rushed over to him expecting the worst, but before I got to him he got up and started walking towards the bike shed. I soon caught up with him.

"Kevin, are you alright?" was the only thing I could think of saying. He turned

"Did you see what happened?" he whispered.

"Of course I did," I replied. "I saw you smash into the concrete path and then get up as if you'd just fallen over. What's going on Kevin? Nobody could survive a fall like that and not have any injuries." He stared at me for a few seconds.

"OK, come around to my place tonight about eight, you are my best friend and you deserve to know. Anyway I will be leaving tomorrow so it won't make any difference."

"Leaving?" I echoed as he got on his bike and pedalled off.

"Just come around tonight and I'll explain," he shouted as he disappeared behind some parked cars. After tea I cycled the one mile to Kevin's house. I was a bit early, but Kevin answered the door and let me in. I was expecting to meet his parents but Kevin was alone.

"Where are your parents Kevin?" I asked. I was not about to be fobbed off with any more excuses.

"I don't have any," he said then he paused, "Well, not here anyway."

I was about to ask him another question when he continued. "I will show you why I cannot be injured by anybody or anything."

I was becoming a bit scared, but Kevin sensing my anxiety continued. "I am not the same as you; I come from another planet in another galaxy. We have been watching the human race over the past year to see if we could live alongside you on this planet. You see in less than a year our planet will collide with a giant meteorite that will destroy our civilisation. We must find another planet before it's too late."

He stopped talking, realizing I was not taking him seriously. I sat down wondering if he was just making all this up to humour me.

"I suppose I will have to prove it before you will believe me" he said. Kevin turned and went into the kitchen, emerging a few seconds later with a large bread knife which he handed to me.

"Go on, try and stab me!" he said. I hesitated, not knowing what to do. "Look, you saw Mark Rusher and his gang beat me up. You saw me fall off the gym roof. Have you ever seen me injured?" I shook my head. "Go on then, I promise you will not harm me." I raised the knife and half-heartedly stabbed him in the arm. The knife seemed to go into something but it was not Kevin's arm, I drew back the knife and plunged it into Kevin's stomach, again he seemed unharmed.

"How is that possible?" I asked, but before I had time to finish the sentence Kevin interrupted. "A forcefield" he said. "I have my own personal forcefield that will automatically sense when I am in danger and protect me, in all of my forty years, I have never been injured."

I interrupted him "Did you say forty years; are you trying to tell me you are forty years old?" Kevin continued. "Yes, on my planet. You see your year is equivalent to five of ours." Kevin paused as he could see I was still not fully convinced.

"I know this sounds crazy," he said, "But I am telling you because you are the only human that has shown me any compassion. I have been here for fifteen of our years and have studied the crucial learning years of the human age span."

I then interrupted him again, there were so many questions I wanted to ask, but the first one that came into my head was "Are there any more like you living here?"

"Yes, there are," replied Kevin with a smile on his face, well I think it was a smile; his face seemed a little contorted as though he was finding it difficult to simulate this natural human activity.

"There are four of us each assigned to research different age groups: children, teenagers, middle aged, and senior. I was selected because I am the same age and roughly the same size as this age group."

"So where are all the others?" I asked.

"They are all close by," replied Kevin. "One is a headmaster of a primary school. One is a scientist working at the Atomic Research Centre, and the other one" he chuckled, "has just been elected as your local MP."

"Are any of them female?" I asked. Kevin chuckled again, and then continued. "Our species do not have different sexes. We are all the same: we have both male and female sex organs. I believe you would call us hermaphrodites."

"I don't understand," I said, feeling rather foolish.

"I know this is hard to believe" said Kevin, "But when I said I was not the same as you, I meant looked like you. This is not my natural body; I can change into any living animal or species that is my size but I am fully grown and will not get any bigger. But you are still growing. That's why I am a bit smaller than most humans your age."

This conversation was way above my head, and I didn't know what to think.

"There is something I can do that will prove I am telling the truth" said Kevin. "I can show you what our species really look like if you want me to. But you will have to be strong and not get frightened. I promise I will not harm you."

"Very well, prove it!" I said, feeling really brave.

"There is one other thing" said Kevin. "I won't be able to speak to you; our species do not have proper vocal cords like humans, so we communicate by thought and touching."

"Ok" I said. "Will it take long?"

"No, but it uses all my strength to transform and takes me a while to recover" replied Kevin. "That is the only time when we are vulnerable. Now sit down and don't be afraid."

Kevin took all his clothes off and then lay on the floor. I watched in amazement as he twisted and convulsed on the floor then slowly his skin started to turn grey and scaly. His arms began to shrink and his legs began to expand. And then a large growth began to form at the base of the spine.

But the biggest change was his head; it grew longer with small pointed ears and an elongated mouth with sharp teeth that protruded over the bottom jaw. The creature lay there exhausted, panting for air, and then it stood up and looked at me. It wasn't any taller or bigger in size than Kevin, but it did look more frightening. It stood on its back legs resting against a tail-like limb, similar to a kangaroo's stance but its body resembled a lizard's. It didn't move, just stared at me. The whole transformation had taken about four minutes.

"OK Kevin, I believe you now" I said, trying not to look it in the eye. It did not reply but seemed to understand; it lay back down on the floor and reversed the transformation. I could see now why Kevin stood so awkwardly, it must have been very uncomfortable changing into a human. Four minutes later Kevin had returned to his human form. He lay still for a few minutes staring at me, hoping I understood what he had done. He stood up made a gargling noise as though he was tuning his vocal cords then said: "Did I frighten you Alan?"

"Yes" I replied "A bit." I didn't know what else to say. Here was my friend who had just turned into some sort of lizard, asking me if I was frightened.

"How did you get here?" I asked.

"We were transported in a beam of light from the mother ship, high up in the outer atmosphere."

"Can't we detect your ship from earth?"

"No" replied Kevin, "We are much more advanced than you, our ship is invisible. Humans will never know we were here."

"But why did you need to come to Earth?" I asked. "Why didn't you just beam up some humans to study them?"

"We do" said Kevin. "We found the best time is when humans are asleep, so we can study them and read their thoughts. Then we return them, and when they wake up it all seems like a dream to them."

"But," I persisted "Why did you have to be here, if you could study us from your ship?"

"Because we needed to be among you" replied Kevin. "To experience your emotions, your reactions to change and to feel the world around us, something you can't get from thoughts."

"And do you think you could live among us?" I asked.

"No," replied Kevin. "You live on a beautiful planet. But you are destroying it."

"You are extracting all its natural resources and cannot feed your own growing population. Humans are an aggressive race, there will never be any peace, and you kill and maim each other constantly with wars and disagreements. This would be much too hostile an environment for us to live amongst you." He stopped talking as if to gather enough strength to continue. "I will answer more of your questions, but they will have to wait until tomorrow." He paused as if reluctant to say any more, and then continued. "That's when we'll be leaving to return to our planet."

"Leaving?" I said "But why?"

"Because we have achieved our objectives, there will be no benefit in staying here any longer, and we still have to find a suitable planet for our species to survive." He looked at his watch. "You will really have to go now, it's getting late and I am feeling very tired."

I could see Kevin was not going to answer any more questions. So I bade him farewell and left.

CHAPTER 3

That night I dreamt about all the things Kevin had told me, it all seemed so incredible, and it wasn't until midday that I woke up.

"You must have been very tired" my mother said when I eventually came down for breakfast. "You were tossing and turning all night, mumbling about Kevin not going back. Is he leaving?" she asked. That brought me to my senses.

"Mum, I have to go" I blurted out. "I may be having a sleepover at Kevin's, so don't wait up."

I rushed out of the door before my mother could interrogate me anymore. In ten minutes I had cycled over to Kevin's house. As I rang the doorbell I thought of all the other questions I would ask Kevin. I pushed the doorbell a second time but there was still no answer. I looked down at my watch, and then had a horrible feeling. Had Kevin already left? Had he slipped something into my tea the night before, knowing I would oversleep, so he could sneak off without anybody knowing? I banged on the front door one more time, but there was still no answer so I left.

It was dusk before I decided to go over to Kevin's and try just one more time. As I was cycling up the road I could see a large estate car parked in Kevin's drive. My heart beat faster, perhaps I hadn't missed him, and maybe he'd overslept like me. I leant my bike against the wall and banged on the front door. At first there was no answer, but I knew somebody was inside. All the curtains were drawn and I was sure there were lights on inside. I pressed my ear to the letterbox and slightly pushed it open. I could just hear people whispering, but not actually what they were saying. Then the door opened suddenly. A smartly dressed man with white hair and a pair of bifocal glasses stood in the doorway.

"What do you want?" he asked rather sharply. "I would like to speak to Kevin, please" I answered in a polite voice.

"He's not here, and I don't know when he will be back," the man replied. "Now, please go away." He went to shut the door, but I put my foot against the frame, stopping him from doing so.

"You're the scientist aren't you?" I said "Don't worry I haven't told anybody." As he hesitated, Kevin poked his head around the corner.

"It's OK" said Kevin, "He's my friend, let him in." The man let the door swing open and I stepped inside and heard the door shut behind me. Kevin led me into the front room where there were two people standing by the settee. I guessed the one on the right was the headmaster of the primary school; he was quite young, with a head full of blonde hair and was dressed smartly but casual. The one on the left was definitely the oldest, his black hair was thinning on the top and he wore thick rimmed glasses He was dressed in a smart suit, and looked familiar, he had to be the MP. The man that had let me in joined them.

"This is my friend Alan" said Kevin. "He knows why we were sent here. He would like to ask some more questions before we go home."

The MP replied "I think you have told him enough Kevin, we don't want to frighten the boy."

"But I have already shown him what we look like" said Kevin.

"You mean you changed?" said the MP, surprised.

"Yes" Kevin replied.

"That was very foolish, what if he had told the police?" said the MP. "You could have jeopardised the whole project." He moved over to the curtains and drew them slightly, expecting to see police cars outside, but it was all clear and already dark.

"Oh, very well!" said the MP. "What questions do you want to ask?" I fumbled in my pocket for the questions I'd written down so I would not forget. I found the scrap of paper and held it up to the light. The others sat down on the settee with Kevin perched on the arm.

"Err um" I cleared my throat and felt all eyes on me "What do you eat?" I asked.

"Mostly green stuff, vegetation that sort of thing." replied the headmaster, "And er, vegetables."

"Do any of you have children?" I asked.

They all looked at each other as if I had asked something very personal. The headmaster spoke first.

"No, we personally do not have any new-borns. Our species usually find a mate and then decide who is going to give birth. Each individual can only give birth once in their lifetime if they choose."

I was going to ask why, but he continued: "When our species give birth, all the reproductive system comes out with the new-born so we cannot reproduce after that." They all seemed a little restless after my questioning and the MP asked if I would like a drink. "We can only offer you water, I'm afraid that is all we drink." I accepted the offer and he disappeared into the kitchen. Then the scientist spoke.

"Aren't you afraid of us?" he said. "After all you've seen what we really look like."

"No," I said. "If you were going to harm me you would have done so by now, anyway I trust Kevin; he hasn't got a violent bone in his body, so I presume you don't either."

The scientist looked surprised and sat back down. The MP came back into the room carrying a tray full of glasses filled with water. After we had finished our drinks, the MP looked at the wall clock.

"I think you need to go now Kevin" he said "We need to prepare for the journey home."

"Could I come and watch you?" I asked, looking at Kevin. He looked at the others for their approval.

"What about your mother?" the headmaster asked. "Won't she be worried?"

"No" I replied. "I told her I was having a sleepover at Kevin's place."

"You seem to have thought of everything" said the MP. "I suppose it will do no harm, but you will have to cycle home on your own late at night."

"Will it be very far?" I asked. The headmaster went over to a drawer in a side cabinet, took out a map of the area and laid it out on the table. He pointed to a series of hills not far from Didcot Town. I recognized them immediately.

"That's Wittenham Clumps!" I cried. "It's only about two miles from my house."

"Very well," said the MP. "We leave in thirty minutes; we can put your bike in the back of the car. Now sit down and wait for us." They all left the room and left me sitting alone on the settee. I suppose I sat there for at least twenty minutes before Kevin reappeared. He was wearing what looked like a crude space suit. It was made of a light green material, but it looked more like a kiddie's romper suit. I tried not to laugh and when Kevin let me feel the material it felt strange, cold and slimy to the touch.

"This is the only material we can wear on the journey," said Kevin. "You see we travel so fast it helps keep our blood cool."

"Well, how fast do you travel?" I asked. "Is it faster than the space shuttle?" I chuckled.

"Much faster" said Kevin "About 100 times the speed of light."

"Well, how fast is that?" I said, knowing science was Kevin's best subject at school. Kevin thought for a while then replied.

"How long does it take for your astronauts to get to your moon?"

"About four days I think" I replied.

"Let me give you a comparison, so you will understand," said Kevin. "If we travelled at the speed of light, then it would take less than 1 second to reach the moon, but we can travel 100 times faster than that." I was about to ask him what was the furthest planet he had been to, when the others came into the room all dressed in the same green outfits.

"We have to go now," said the MP looking at the wall clock. They all left the house. Kevin locked the front door and put the key through the letterbox. If anybody had seen them now it looked like they were going to a fancy dress party, dressed as frogs. But there was nobody about. The head teacher put my bike in the back of the estate car and we all set off with me sitting between the MP and Kevin. The scientist sat in the passenger seat and the Headmaster was driving. It didn't take long before we had reached the car park at Wittenham Clumps. They each took a small object in their hand, and left the car.

I followed them up the highest hill, until we reached the top. They spread out about ten feet apart, and then placed the objects at their feet. I presume they were some sort of homing beacon. I was standing about twenty feet away. It was a full moon so I could see them quite clearly. The MP waved, then there was a flash of light and in the blink of an eye he was gone. Seconds later another flash and the scientist disappeared. The headmaster was about to wave, but he too disappeared. Kevin just had time to say "Goodbye!" before there was another flash and they were all gone.

It had taken maybe eight seconds altogether. I looked up into the clear sky and suddenly saw a shooting star before it disappeared. I wondered if that was my friend Kevin, on his way home. I ran back down the hill, took my bike out of the car and rode home. I had my own key so I let myself in and went to bed; it was 1 o' clock before I closed my eyes and fell asleep.

The next day there were some reports of lightning flashes seen on Wittenham Clumps around midnight, and the police found an abandoned hire car left at the car park, but the driver was never traced.

UPTON STATION

CHAPTER 1

My father, William Norris, had worked on the railways since 1954. He started as a porter, ferrying people's luggage up and down the platforms on his little red sack trolley. Then he progressed to guardsman, travelling at the rear of the train in the guard's van. He really wanted to be a steam engine driver, but had never quite made the grade. However, he loved his job, jumping off the guard's van as the train pulled into the station and opening the doors for the passengers. He worked at the newly revamped Didcot Parkway these days, but back then it was just called Didcot Station. He often travelled from Didcot to Newbury on the old branch line.

I suppose I was about six or seven when Dad began to tell me stories about the old branch line. He always confided in me rather than my older brother; although two years older than me, Martin was never very close to my father. He was always a Mummy's boy, and would run to his mother if he fell over or wanted some sympathy. Perhaps he was scared of Dad; he was quite a strict man and didn't think twice about giving you a clip around the ear if you cheeked him. But to me he was my hero. He'd come in smelling of smoke and coal, even though he wasn't an engine driver. I think he often climbed up into the cab while waiting at the station and helped stoke up the fire. Even back then he was quite a large man for his five feet six frame, completely the opposite of Mum's slim, petite figure.

We lived in the railway cottages down Station Road. It wasn't a particularly nice house, but it was convenient for

Dad's work, being only five hundred yards from the station. One evening we were all sitting around the kitchen table eating, we always had our main meal in the evening after Dad arrived home. I remember him telling us about a young girl of about five, dressed in a distinctive red coat. She was holding her mother's hand. Dad was on the other platform and she waved to him, so Dad waved back. She slipped out of her mother's hand without her realizing and walked towards him. In horror Dad shouted, "Look out!"

Everybody looked around at him, but it was too late. The girl walked off the edge of the platform just as a train thundered through the station. My Dad screamed "Oh my God!" and buried his face in his hands. He looked up when the train had passed, expecting to see the little mangled body of the girl lying on the track. But she wasn't, she was still standing with her mother clutching her hand. Dad stood there open-mouthed, and then noticed everybody was watching him. It had looked so real; had he imagined it all? He felt a bit embarrassed and carried on with his work. But the strange thing was two days later a little girl with a red coat fell off the platform and was killed by a passing train.

The incident unsettled Dad for a few days as nobody would believe his premonition. That was the earliest incident I can remember. Then, about a year later, Dad was traveling along the old branch line to Newbury. There were two tracks by then, one for passengers going to Newbury and the other was for freight, mainly to serve the large Army Depot at Milton, just outside Didcot.

The old passenger steam train rattled along the bumpy track passing through Upton Station. Just beyond the station, the line curved into a deep cutting passing through fields. Dad had been promoted to senior guardsman by then and was standing on the small rear platform of the guard's van looking down the side of the train. A small freight train was coming towards him and he thought he might wave to the driver as it passed him. As the train got closer Dad realized just how fast it was going. It shot past; Dad didn't even have time to see the driver, let alone wave at him. He turned around and watched as the train rounded the curve. There was a screeching of brakes as the train and freight wagons came off the track and came to rest in a crumpled mess blocking the tracks. Dad immediately pulled the emergency cord and the train slowed down to a stop. Dad ran along the carriages and through the frightened passengers. He climbed out of the last carriage and went alongside the engine; the driver leaned out and asked what the emergency was. Dad explained that there had been a terrible accident. The freight train that just passed had derailed on the Upton curve. The train driver looked down at my father as if he were bonkers.

"What train?" he asked.

"The freight train," my father screamed. "Come on, we must see if the driver needs help!" He ran back up the track, closely followed by the fireman and driver. The curve was a good hundred yards back up the track. Dad raced around the curve and stopped. He stared in disbelief, but there was no train. No freight wagons were blocking the track. The driver and fireman caught my father up, breathing heavily. They looked up and down the track, and then looked at my father.

"Is this some sort of joke?" said the driver, "Because if it is, it's not very funny." He looked at his watch. "Because of you we are now over half an hour behind schedule." They turned and made their way back to the train, with Dad trailing behind trying to figure out what had just happened.

He was reported for pulling the emergency cord and stopping the train for no reason. Even though he swore on oath that he had seen the train crash nobody believed him. But, because he had worked for the railways for a long time, he was let off with a caution. Four weeks later a freight train did come off the rails at the Upton Curve, blocking the track for a short while. Ned Rogers, the engine driver, was thrown out of the cab and died instantly and Charlie Brown, the fireman, died in hospital the next day. But it wasn't speed that derailed the train; it was an unsecured joint in the track that had come apart. Everybody had forgotten that Dad had predicted the accident a month before, believing it was just a coincidence.

In the early sixties Dr Beeching, the Government Minister in charge of the railways, undertook a major transformation of the rail network which was losing money. He closed hundreds of small stations and branch lines that were not profitable, causing mass unemployment. By then Dad had been promoted to ticket collector, working on the main line between Didcot and Paddington, but the old branch line between Didcot and Newbury was closed. The freight line stayed open for a few more years, but that too was eventually closed. Dad didn't actually predict any more incidents, but it didn't stop him from telling me stories about some imaginary people and objects he had seen on the railway. It was about this time that two of my Dad's mates died within weeks of each other.

First Tom, the old engine driver who used to operate the large steam trains on the Didcot to Paddington line, died after climbing down from the cab while in the station. He slipped and fell, smashing his head on the platform. My Dad saw it happen and rushed over to help him. He put his jacket under his head and held his hand. Tom, with blood streaming down his forehead, just said four words: "See you later, mate." He closed his eyes and then died. The ambulance arrived, soon after, but there was nothing anybody could do. It was discovered later he had died from a massive brain haemorrhage. Then Dave, another ticket collector that Dad had known for years, died suddenly from a heart attack. Dad was in the station canteen having a drink of tea with him when he clutched his heart, made a few gasps, rolled his eyes then fell off his seat and died. A few years later Dad said he had seen Dave seating in the canteen in the same seat. He waved to Dad. My father went over to him, not believing his eyes. But as he got nearer the apparition faded then disappeared.

I had grown up and got married by this time. We moved away from the area and bought a nice house in Basingstoke. I didn't see Dad very often from then on. He still worked on the railways, but people had noticed he was becoming very forgetful and not knowing where he was sometimes. Not long after there were more cuts to the rail network. Trains no longer needed guards' vans and they were gradually phased out. Because of his age and decline in health Dad was offered a job in the station sweeping up and generally keeping the station clean, a bit of a demeaning job, but Dad was sixty four and only had to work for another year before he could retire, so he took the job.

The following month Mum died of cancer and Dad never really recovered from that. He moved out of the cottage in Station Road, the house in which he had lived all of his married life, and moved into sheltered accommodation. Dad retired ten months later. By this time I had a four year old boy named Peter and my little girl Rosie, aged three. I felt guilty about living so far away from Dad. My older brother, Martin, had got married several years earlier and moved to Devon, so he had no immediate family living close by. My wife and I decided to move back to Didcot to be closer to Dad, with the intention of buying a bigger house, so he could move in with us. After months of searching with no luck, my wife tried the internet and called out to me one evening.

"Alan, come quickly!" I raced upstairs and into the bedroom. "Look at this," she said. "Remember the old Upton Station just outside Didcot?"

I nodded. "Well, it's up for sale." I quickly read through the advert. "It's rather small and hasn't been lived in for ten years," I replied. "It will need a lot of renovation work."

"But," my wife argued, "You're a builder, you could easily build an extension and do the place up a bit." She paused. "And wouldn't this be a great place for your father to live, it will bring back all his old memories of the railway?" I thought the suggestion through and agreed with my wife. The next day I went along to Lester's, the local estate agent and spoke to the manager.

"It's not reached the asking price yet" he said. "But we have had an offer on it." He looked at me and winked. "If you offered the asking price, then I think the seller would accept." So that morning I offered the asking price and by lunchtime Upton station was mine. My wife was delighted. Four weeks later everything had been settled, and I had the keys.

"Let's go out to see the property right now," I suggested when I arrived home. My wife couldn't wait and half an hour later we were standing outside Upton Station. It wasn't quite as bad as I had expected. The roof was still intact and the interior was dry, apart from a few damp patches in the corners, but it was very old fashioned and had not been modernized or decorated for at least fifty years. I was already imagining how it would look after I had built the extension and knocked down a few walls. We both went outside and stood on the platform. The railway lines and sleepers had been removed years ago, but you could still see where the track used to be. Our property had been fenced off and beyond that most of the old track had been converted into tarmac paths by the local council. It was possible to walk to Didcot along the embankments with stunning views over the surrounding countryside and the path was very popular with dog walkers and ramblers. We stood there for some time in the afternoon sunshine gazing over the surrounding fields, and I wondered whether I had made the right decision.

The next day Dad was taken into hospital for some tests and a few days later we had a letter confirming he had the early stages of Alzheimer's disease. So it was imperative that I got started on Upton Station straight away. I went along to my local bank and arranged a bridging loan, as I didn't have the finances to start until our house had been sold. We started renovating the existing station. After three months we had planning permission for the new extension and six months later we had finished.

"Now we can all move in together," my wife said. "We must bring Dad over tomorrow and show him his ground floor bedroom." It couldn't have come any sooner, Dad was getting worse and he could no longer look after himself. He loved the station, and after a couple of weeks he seemed to be improving. He would sit out on the old platform in his tatty old deckchair listening to the distant trains pulling in and out of Didcot Station. Although the station was just over a mile away, on a nice day with the wind in the right direction, they were quite distinct.

"That's a two four two class," my Dad said one afternoon as we were all sitting sunbathing on the platform. "That's one of the large trains that I used to drive up to London." Peter was by Dad's side listening intently to what he was saying. I looked over to my wife with raised eyebrows.

"Dad, stop exaggerating!" I said. "You didn't actually drive the trains yourself, did you?"

"Oh, didn't I?" Dad replied. "Well, how did the trains get up to London then?"

I looked at him directly and said "You were a ticket collector, remember? Somebody else drove the trains." I felt a bit guilty about correcting him in front of the family, but he didn't seem to mind and rambled on about what he had seen on the trains and then suddenly cried out. "Why doesn't anybody believe me anymore?"

Peter who had been studying Dad's face said "I believe you, Granddad." I didn't make any comment, but realised Dad hadn't improved.

A few weeks later I noticed he was confiding in Peter more and more. I caught him whispering into Peter's ear one evening, and asked him what he had said. "Oh it's nothing, Dad," Peter replied. "He just said he may be going away soon and I was not to worry."

"Peter," I replied, trying not to frighten the boy. "Granddad's not very well, and will gradually get worse. Don't believe everything he tells you. He sometimes exaggerates the truth; he's old and sometimes doesn't know what he is saying."

Peter seemed to understand my explanation, and very soon the incident was forgotten. I tried to make Dad's life as comfortable and interesting as possible and often took him along to the open days at Didcot Railway Centre. He loved it there, the twinkle seemed to come back into his eyes, especially if one of his friends recognised him and made some conservation. But the highlight of the day was a trip in one of the carriages that took tourists up and down the track towards Appleford. He would sit quietly in a corner blankly staring at all the other passengers. Then one day as we were returning home in the car he said "Did you see them son, all the dead people?" I slammed on the brakes, luckily there was nobody behind me or I would have been shunted in the rear. I looked around at him sitting in the back seat with an emotional stare.

"What dead people?" I asked.

"The dead people in the carriage," he replied. This answer completely took me by surprise and for a moment I didn't know what to say.

"Dad, I was with you the whole time and I didn't see any dead people, there were only tourists in the carriage. You must have imagined them."

He didn't reply, he just closed his eyes and pretended he was asleep. I told my wife as soon as we got home.

"I think Dad needs to see a specialist, he seems to be getting worse. He told me today he could see dead people." My wife was concerned and we arranged for Dad to see a psychiatrist the following week. After examining him and asking him a series of questions, the psychiatrist took me to one side out of earshot from Dad.

"I am afraid your father has senile dementia," said the psychiatrist. "There's not a lot we can do. But these might help." He reached down and pulled a drawer open, took out a small jar of tablets and handed them to me. "Give him two of these a day, one in the morning and one in the evening, they should calm him down. Keep a close eye on him though because there may be some side effects."

"Side effects," I replied concerned. "What side effects?"

"They're steroid tablets," the psychiatrist said. "They may give him headaches or make him sick. But most patients benefit from them."

I thanked him and then helped Dad to his feet. He was a bit unsteady walking down the stairs, but I managed to get him into the car and we drove home. Dad did seem to get better for a while and on his good days you could have a sensible conversation with him. On his bad days, however, he was just a mumbling wreck.

A few days later I woke up, got dressed and went outside. The weather was glorious with not a cloud in the sky.

"I reckon it will be hot today," I said to my wife who had joined me on the platform. "I think I'll walk to Didcot along the old embankment, and perhaps do a bit of shopping. I'll ask Dad, Peter and Rosie if they want to come." My wife agreed, but when I asked Rosie she didn't seem interested.

"You only talk about trains" she said, "And that's boring!" So I left her playing with her dolls. But Dad and Peter were keen. It was one of Dad's better days, he seemed to be on the ball and the old twinkle was back in his eyes. We pushed through the gap in the fence at the bottom of the garden and set off along the old train track towards Didcot. We met a few ramblers along the way. One was walking his dog, Dad bent down to stroke it, but it growled so he stood back up.

"That's strange" said the man. "She's so placid I have never heard her growl at anybody before." He pulled on the dog's lead and hurried off down the path. We were about halfway along the track. Dad was leading, I was following and Peter was lagging along behind as usual. I glanced around, the cows were grazing in the fields, the air was still and it felt good to be alive. Then Dad suddenly stopped, he put his arm out sideways to prevent me from passing.

"Wait," he said. "I think there's a train coming." I listened, but could not hear anything. I looked behind at Peter who was still some way behind and beckoned him to hurry up.

Then Dad said "Quick, stand to the side!" He pushed me and Peter to the side of the embankment. I stood there looking along the old railway embankment. Then I felt a chill wind whistle past me and the faint smell of smoke. I looked at Dad, his white hair blowing in the wind and suddenly the sensation was gone.

"Come on," he said. "Let's get going before another train comes." Then he carried on walking up the track. I didn't make any comment, but looked at Pete.

"Did you feel that, Pete?" I asked. He looked a bit frightened and nodded. I grabbed his hand and we followed Dad along the track.

We walked around Didcot browsing in the shops, had a drink of tea in one of the cafes, bought a few things then returned home along the same path. There were no eerie sensations on the way back, but we did walk a lot faster. I mentioned it to my wife later in bed, but either she was very tired and didn't want to talk, or she just wasn't interested, so I dropped the subject.

CHAPTER 2

One morning Peter came over to me, as I was writing at my desk and whispered into my ear. "Granddad's packed his suitcase and is catching the twelve o'clock train. Don't tell him I told you, it's supposed to be a secret."

"Okay Peter, I won't say a word," I replied. "Thanks for telling me."

He seemed happy that he had told somebody and scampered off outside. I looked out from my bedroom window overlooking the platform. I could see Dad sitting in his old deckchair, he seemed to be asleep. So I sneaked down and crept into his bedroom on the ground floor. The bedroom was remarkably clean and tidy with his bed made. I noticed a small green suitcase standing beside the bed. I picked it up, put it on the bed and opened it. There was not much inside: a neatly folded pair of trousers, a shirt and cardigan, some underwear, a pair of socks and his favourite pair of shoes. He couldn't have got anything else in the suitcase if he had tried, it was full. I put all the things back as neatly as possible, closed the suitcase and placed it back beside the bed. I glanced out of the back door. Dad was still sound asleep in his deckchair. I looked at my watch; it was only ten forty five. But I decided to keep an eye on him anyway, just in case the old man tried to do something silly. My wife walked past me in the hallway.

"Did you clean Dad's bedroom this morning?" I shouted after her. A few seconds later her head appeared around the door

"No, you know I always clean his room in the evening, why do you ask?"

"Oh, nothing important," I replied. But was it important? Why had dad cleaned his room, he'd never done it before, and why was his suitcase packed? I glanced at my watch again: eleven thirty. I decided to wake him up and ask him what he was up to. He was still asleep as I approached him. I gently shook him on his shoulder.

"Wake up Dad, it's twelve thirty!" expecting to get a reaction with him leaping out of the deck chair shouting "I'm late, I'm late!" But he opened his eyes and looked at me.

"Oh, there's plenty of time yet," he muttered. Then he closed his eyes and promptly went back to sleep. I let him sleep; at least he was not going anywhere at twelve o' clock. It was probably all in his imagination, and then I wondered if the tablets were making him hallucinate. They did seem to give him plenty of rest and there didn't seem to be any other side effects.

That night my wife and I went to bed early as we were both extremely tired. Peter and Rosie had been in bed by eight, and I had said goodnight to Dad at around ten, after checking he was safely tucked up in bed. I glanced around the bedroom but couldn't see the little green suitcase. I closed the door and crept back into my bedroom. My wife was already asleep so I decided not to question her about dad's tidy room and the disappearance of the little green suitcase. It could wait until the morning. So I curled up next to my wife and fell asleep.

I suppose it was about eleven thirty when I was awoken by the noise of steam trains shunting back and forth. I was still a bit groggy but wasn't surprised at the noise. Didcot Station sometimes worked quite late into the night getting all the rolling stock ready for the morning. So I rolled over and put my pillow over my head and gradually slipped into a light sleep. Suddenly I was being shaken vigorously.

"Wake up, Dad, wake up!" Peter was shaking me.

"What's the matter, son?" I asked, not fully awake.

"It's Granddad, he's waiting outside on the platform with his suitcase," Peter said. "I think he's leaving." This woke me up instantly; I got out of bed, slipped on my dressing gown and followed Peter on to the platform outside. Dad was standing at the far end of the platform with the little green suitcase, just as Peter had said. It was a pleasant evening and I could still hear the steam engines in the distance, but they seemed to be getting louder. I looked up at the station clock: eleven fifty five, then it dawned on me; it was twelve o 'clock midnight that Dad was talking about. I looked down the track towards Didcot and could just make out a bright light coming towards us. At first I thought it might be a helicopter, but that theory was soon dashed as the light was so close to the ground. A hand suddenly grasped mine and made me jump.

"What's happening, darling?" my wife said in a sleepy voice. "Why is your Dad standing on the platform in his dressing gown?" By this time Rosie had slipped out and was holding her mother's hand.

"Where is Granddad going?" she whispered. But nobody answered her; we were all too busy watching the train getting closer and closer. I knew it was impossible, because there were no tracks. But the train was still getting closer; it seemed to be hovering just above the ground. Peter squeezed my hand.

"Is it coming for Granddad?" he whispered.

"I don't know, son," I said softly. "Let's just wait and see."

I couldn't take my eyes off the train. Suddenly the still night was broken by a shrill whistle and the screeching of brakes as the steam engine burst through the smoke and stopped at Upton Station. The station clock had just turned midnight. We were all standing in a group holding hands; my wife squeezed mine harder just to make sure she wasn't dreaming. But we could all see the ashen faces staring at us through the carriage windows. I recognized some of the people: Ned the engine driver, Charlie the fireman, Dave the ticket collector and old Tom, Dad's friend who drove the large trains up to London. And there in the end widow, a little girl in a red coat waving frantically. But none of them were frightening or scary, they were all smiling.

I looked over at Dad; he was shaking hands with the ghostlike figure of the engine driver then he walked past both carriages not looking at us. I shouted as he climbed the step into the last carriage, but he didn't hear us. We saw him walk down the aisle and sit next down next to an old lady. I recognized her immediately: it was my mother and she was smiling. Then they both started waving. So we all waved back, it must have looked funny, my whole family dressed in dressing gowns waving at ghosts. Suddenly a man jumped out of the guard's van at the rear of the carriages. He blew his whistle and shouted. "All aboard!" and then he waved his green flag.

The train lurched forward and began slowly leaving the station. Everybody was still waving as the train disappeared around the Upton Curve and suddenly it was gone. We all stood there for a few minutes before Peter spoke out.

"Will we ever see Granddad again?"

"I don't think so, Peter," I replied with tears welling up in my eyes. "I think he's gone to heaven."

We all made our way back indoors and went to bed. I had a quick look in Dad's bedroom just to make sure I hadn't dreamt the whole thing. The bed was neatly made, but there was no sign of him. I was just about to close the door when I spotted a white envelope lying on the pillow. I went across and picked it up. Written across the front in capital letters were three words: TO MY SON. I quickly tore the envelope open and took out the letter. It read:

I WISH YOU HAD BELIVED ME SON, BUT IT'S TOO LATE NOW. I HAVE GONE TO A BETTER PLACE. GIVE MY LOVE TO ALL THE FAMILY, LOVE DAD.

I could not hold on to my emotions any longer and burst into tears. I lay on Dad's bed and cried myself to sleep. The next morning it all seemed a hazy memory. None of my family spoke much at the breakfast table, all trying to understand what had happened. Then I spoke:

"I suppose we will have to inform the police about Dad." My wife looked at me disbelievingly.

"What are you going to tell them?" she asked. "That your father was whisked away by a ghost train?"

"Perhaps you are right," I replied. "I'll just tell them he is missing; nobody would believe us any way." Those words haunted me and then I remembered the letter. I got up and showed it to my wife.

"It's not your fault, darling," she whispered after she had read the letter. "Nobody believed him."

That morning I reported Dad missing at the local Police Station, as this seemed the right thing to do. The police took all the necessary information and seemed very sympathetic. But deep down I knew I was wasting their time, and they would never find him.

THE TRACTOR

CHAPTER 1

The McDonalds and the Clevelands owned the biggest farms in Oxfordshire. There had been a long running feud between the two families for years; no one knew exactly how it had begun. Some say it was over land rights, others say it all started after the affair between Amy McDonald, Shaun McDonald's wife and Josh Cleveland the son of Jessica Cleveland. Although it started a long time ago, and the offenders had been dead some twenty years, there was still tension between the two families, each trying to outdo the other.

If I were to choose who was the richest and biggest, then probably it was the McDonalds. Stuart McDonald the present owner was the most ruthless penny-pinching boss as anybody who had the misfortune to work for him soon discovered. Over the last thirty years he had reduced his farmworkers from twenty seven to just three. The workers lived in tied cottages and most had a wife and children. But if he could save money by buying newer, more modern equipment which eliminated or reduced farm staff then he had no hesitation in evicting them and then selling the cottages. That's why the lucky three, if you could call them lucky, worked their socks off just to keep a roof over their heads.

Alfie Bates was one of the lucky three. He had a wife and three children, all under seven. It was hard living on the meagre wages that Stuart McDonald paid them. Alfie was a very good tractor driver who also drove the huge combine harvester in the summer. He worked long hours, often late into the night, and would come home exhausted.

"You're working too hard" said his wife Patti, "at this rate you will be dead before you get to thirty." Alfie slumped into his favourite armchair by the fire and sighed. "I know, but do I have any choice? The jobs around here are very scarce. Most of the farms are reducing their staff and I have to think of you and the kids. At least we have a home." Patti knelt down next to him and gave him a hug.

"I know dear, I just wish your boss was not so tight and gave you a bonus now and again."

Stuart McDonald was up bright and early the next morning. As the three farm workers walked through the yard gate, he called them over.

"I have some good news and some bad news for you," he said. "As you know, all our tractors are getting old and need a lot of maintenance. My local agricultural suppliers have offered me a brand new tractor for a year, with the option of buying the tractor at half price after this period. It's fitted with the latest technology and will require one of you to take a week's course on the driving procedures," he paused and chuckled to himself. "All paid for by the distributors, of course. The bad news is the tractor can do the work of two ordinary tractors;" he paused again, "So one of you will have to leave."

All the men looked at each other in despair and it was Alfie who spoke first. "But sir, couldn't you find some maintenance work around the farm? We're all pretty handy with tools." Stuart interrupted Alfie, before he could do any more grovelling.

"I'm sorry, but I need to sell a cottage to pay for the tractor at the end of the year." Then he added, "These tractors aren't cheap, you know. I'll let you decide who stays and who goes.

Now get back to work!" The men drifted off and set about their various chores.

Over the next week it was decided Ray Woods and his wife were to leave. Although his wife was heavily pregnant, they were the latest couple to be employed, as well as the youngest, and they had no other offspring. So it was the obvious choice, much to the relief of Alfie and his wife. Stuart McDonald decided it would be Alfie who took the driving course as he was the oldest and best experienced, but he soon pointed out there would be no increase in wages for driving the new tractor.

CHAPTER 2

Two weeks later the tractor arrived, along with the local press who Stuart McDonald had informed, just to let the Clevelands know that it was the McDonalds who had the latest and newest tractor. It came on the back of the biggest lorry Alfie had ever seen, accompanied by other farm machinery. The driving instructor and a technician drove up a short time later in a Landrover. Alfie stared at the huge tractor as it was being unloaded, and he felt a little bit intimidated by the sheer size of it. When the driver had left the vehicle Alfie walked around the bright green tractor. High up on the side of the engine cover he noticed the yellow lettering: JOHN DEERE 9639 T EXP.

"What do the initials stand for?" he asked the technician who had joined him.

"The 9639 is the model number, the T means tracked and the EXP," he paused. "The EXP means it's experimental." Alfie looked at him, surprised.

"Experimental," he said quietly, "what do you mean by experimental?"

"Alfie, that's your name isn't it?" asked the technician.

"Yes" replied Alfie.

"Well, this tractor" continued the technician, "is the most powerful and advanced tractor in the world. Some of the technology has not been fully tested and we don't know what will work and what will not, under farm conditions, that's why we want you to test it for us over the year. Each month you will fill in a questionnaire, as to the reliability and advantage each component has."

He could see Alfie was becoming a little anxious. "Don't worry, all the questions are quite straightforward. It's only a matter of ticks and crosses and points out of ten, you won't have to write anything." He looked at his watch. "It's getting late, go home and get a good rest we can start the driving course tomorrow." Alfie hesitated. "Go on" he continued "we're paying for your time now."

Alfie didn't have to be told a second time; he was off like a shot. This was the earliest he had finished all year and he didn't want to waste any free time off around a muddy farmyard.

The next morning he was up early, but he realised he could have had an extra three hours in bed as the driving instructor and technician didn't arrive until after nine am.

"Right" said Paul the driving instructor, "I can see you're keen to start. Here you will need this to unlock the cab." He handed Alfie a small remote key fob. They climbed the ladder up into the cab and there was just enough room for Paul to stand behind the seat.

"The glass windows in this cab are virtually unbreakable" said Paul. "If by chance the tractor did topple over on to its side and all the power failed, which has never happened yet" said Paul, "There is a small escape hatch in the roof." He pointed up to a small oblong trap door in the cab roof. "Just twist the manual lock and you will be able to get out."

He then flipped over the seat to reveal all the on-board circuits, and memory banks. Masses of cables fed into the hard drive unit set in the floor below.

"This is the heart of the tractor" said Paul. "All your commands and instructions are recorded and stored here."

"There isn't much room to work on anything" said Alfie.

"No," replied Paul "We have to remove the seat to work on any of the components. But this was the only place we could fit it all in." He slid the seat back into place, and continued "Go on, take a seat!" Alfie slid into the voluptuous, self-adjusting seat. Big side armrests slid onto his thighs, holding him tightly in place. It was more comfortable than his old armchair. His eyes immediately glanced over the mass of switches and buttons, which were quite intimidating.

"Right, let's start by programing your name and voice into the computer," said Paul. He lent over Alfie and pressed a few buttons on the keyboard, now say your name." Alfie froze. "Go on," said Paul "Just say: my name is Alfie." Alfie did as he was told.

"There, that's done" said Paul after pressing a few more keys. "You see, Alfie," Paul continued, "most demands are voice activated and if the computer does not recognize your voice then it will not obey your command."

"You mean I have to tell the tractor what to do by talking to it?" said Alfie amazed.

"Well yes, basically," replied Paul. "It will remember everything you tell it to do. You still have to press a few buttons and switches before commands, and you still have to steer it and control the throttle and foot brake. But once you have ploughed the field the tractor will save all the coordinates and data and the next time it will be able to steer and drive itself. Come on, we'll connect up the plough and then you can drive me to the field."

Alfie backed the tractor up to the biggest plough he had ever seen. It had ten furrows held up by two wheels at the back, but it also had another ten furrows on the top.

"It's reversible" said Paul. "So you can switch it over and go back down the same furrow." Paul showed Alfie how to connect up the plough using the voice control, then he set off down the lane into the field. Two hours later they stopped for lunch and, after another two hours, they finished the lesson.

"I wish I could work for you fulltime!" said Alfie as they were parking the tractor in the barn.

"Someday you might," Paul replied. "You're a quick learner; I don't think you will need a week to complete the course." Paul was right; after just three days Alfie had learnt everything there was to know about the JOHN DEERE 9639 T EXP.

After the instructors had left, Stuart McDonald did not miss a trick. Instead of letting him have the rest of the paid week off, he insisted Alfie start back the next day. So on the Thursday morning at seven am, Alfie climbed into the John Deere cab and sat down. It felt strange, all alone in charge of the most advanced tractor ever built. He looked around the cab and found a small toolbox by the side of his seat.

He opened it up and found spanners, pliers, wire cutters, screwdrivers, a hammer and a small torch all set out in separate trays. On the other side of the seat a small fire extinguisher was neatly strapped to the side of his seat. All were in arm's reach, just in case of any emergencies as the technician had pointed out. He sat up and looked at the mass of switches, dials, buttons and levers. Panic set in, he started to sweat, and then a soft voice spoke to him.

"Good morning, Alfie," the intercom said. "What are we doing today?" For a few seconds Alfie was speechless; he wasn't expecting the tractor to talk to him.

"Good morning, John," was the only thing he thought of saying, after all it was called a JOHN DEERE and the name seemed appropriate. He felt a bit more relaxed and said "Start your engine."

The massive tractor's diesel engine burst into life. Alfie drove around and hitched up the rollers, then drove over to the newly ploughed field. The rollers were used to break up all the large clods of dirt and by midday the whole field had been finished. He then returned to the yard and hitched up the harrows. This time he let the tractor drive itself, keeping his hands just above the steering wheel in case the tractor decided to take a short cut through the hedge. But the tractor did everything perfectly. When they returned to the barn and Alfie was just about to order the tractor to turn of the engine, when a voice came through intercom.

"How did I do today, Alfie?" John asked.

"You did just fine, John," said Alfie. "Now turn off your engine." The tractor cut its engine and fell silent. Alfie climbed down the ladder and pressed the remote control. After the locking system was activated he took one last look at the massive tractor, and then went home to his wife.

CHAPTER 3

Everything was running like clockwork at the McDonalds' farm. Each month Alfie filled in the questionnaire as instructed, which he found easy as most of the boxes just needed a perfect score of 10. But Stuart was pushing Alfie harder and harder, even though they were doing twice as much work. The tractor was never allowed to stay still. Alfie ate, drank and sometimes slept in the cab. Stuart McDonald even made Alfie screw a sign board on the front of the tractor, saying: FOR HIRE ring 01235 832938. Then he started hiring Alfie and the tractor out to other smaller farms just to make even more money for himself.

"We've got to make that tractor pay for itself," was the only answer Stuart gave when Alfie complained about the long hours he was working.

Jim Cleveland, the owner of the other big farm across the valley was furious. "He's taking all the extra work from the other farms," complained Jim to the other farmers down at the local pub. "He'll put us all out of business with that damn tractor."

It was the start of October when the weather changed for the worse; it rained for weeks, flooding the fields. But that didn't stop the JOHN DEERE 9639 T EXP. It ploughed through the soil as if it was ploughing through butter, its massive tracks biting deep into the ground for extra grip. Alfie had instructed the tractor to plough the top field, and, as he snuggled back in to the cosy seat, he told the radio to switch on to Radio 3 and then he relaxed to the sounds of Beethoven.

The rain was still lashing down against the windshield and he could see thunder and lightning in the distance. It was getting dark, but he thought if he finished this field Stuart would be pleased and he could ask him for a pay rise.

He was just dozing when there was a loud crack, a bright light hit the tractor and it stopped dead. All the instruments went out and the computer panel went blank. It was pitch black outside. He fumbled around for the torch in the toolbox at the side of his seat, but couldn't find it. He suddenly felt afraid as if the darkness was closing in on him. The dark cab felt very claustrophobic, as if it was getting smaller and smaller and then crushing him.

He was just about to scream when his hand gripped the torch, but before he could illuminate the eeriness, everything switched itself back on. Music filled the air, the tractor burst into life and the lights came back on. Alfie sank back into his chair, globules of sweat running down his face, but something didn't feel right. He looked around the cab; everything seemed the same.

"John, are you alright?" he asked. He waited a few minutes but there was no reply, he repeated the question; there was still no reply. His thoughts went back to the bright light and loud crack. We must have been struck by lightning, and that's damaged the voice control, was the only conclusion he could come to. Just when he was about to take over the controls, a voice spoke: "I'm alright, some of my circuits are burnt but I can bypass them."

Alfie sat very still, that wasn't John's normal calm voice; the tone was quite sinister.

"John, you sound different, are you sure everything is working OK?"

Again there was no response for a few minutes. Finally the voice said, "Yes, everything is fine and working well. Can we go home now?"

Alfie had never heard John actually ask this type of question before, and knew something was seriously wrong. If he could get the tractor back to the farm, maybe Paul could look at it the next day.

"Yes, we can go home," Alfie said in the most relaxed voice he could find. "We can finish the field off tomorrow." He switched to manual, took over the steering wheel and headed back to the farm. Everything worked as before, apart from the changed voice. He felt a bit more at ease as he locked the tractor and set off the hundred yards or so to his home.

CHAPTER 4

Alfie didn't report the lightning strike to Paul, there didn't seem any point. The JOHN DEERE 9639 T EXP had followed all of Alfie's commands, and John's normal voice had returned. The only difference was that sometimes the sinister voice replied, and occasionally asked some strange questions which hadn't been programed into the computer. It didn't worry Alfie, he just assumed the lightning bolt had scrambled some of John's programming and jumbled them up a bit.

At the end of the year Stuart McDonald had sold the spare cottage and paid off the tractor. Everybody was pleased at the way the tractor had performed, without any reliability problems.

The first few months of the New Year flew by, and it was in March when Alfie first noticed a few changes in John's attitude. The tractor's memory had grown considerably and the voice would sometimes question his commands. But it hadn't disobeyed him, just disagreed with him sometimes.

It was mid-April when Jim Cleveland decided to take revenge on Stuart McDonald. He would hurt him where it hurt the most; he would sabotage his damn tractor. His plan was to sneak up at night and pour sugar into the diesel tank, failing that he would pour water into the oil filler cap. The night he picked was Alfie's birthday party down at the Royal Oak.

He knew Alfie would finish early so he could enjoy the celebrations. Even his penny pinching boss would be there, expecting to get a free drink. That night, as most of the surrounding farm workers joined in the celebrations, Jim crept up to the tractor shed. It wasn't much of a shed only a tin roof and back held up by twelve huge telegraph poles.

There were three bays, the sides were open to the elements. He could see the little Massey Fergusson in one bay; the second bay was occupied by an old Fortson Major; and in the third bay stood the massive John Deere tractor, illuminated in the moonlight. He felt a bit frightened, as if the tractor was watching his every move. A chill swept over him as he climbed up the tractor's ladder. He couldn't see the diesel filler cap and guessed it was inside the cab. He tried the cab door but it was locked, even with a bit of brute force it wouldn't budge. So he walked along the huge tracks looking for the oil filler cap.

When he found the filler cap, he had to lean right inside the engine to reach it. Suddenly the huge engine sputtered into life and the tracks he was standing on began to move. Jim lost his balance and fell backwards on to the ground. He lay there for a few minutes looking up at the giant wooden poles that were supporting the tractor shed. He hadn't noticed them before; they looked menacing, like soldiers standing to attention waiting for something to happen. He tried to stand up, but his leg hurt too much. He crawled over to the cowshed wall and pushed himself upright. Suddenly all the front lights on the tractor flashed on, blinding him. Jim raised his arm to shield his eyes. He sensed the tractor was moving towards him. The next thing Jim felt was the huge two ton ballast bar at the front of the tractor pressing into his ribs. The tractor moved slowly forward, pinning him against the wall of the cowshed.

He screamed "Stop, stop you're crushing me!" but no one heard his pitiful cries. The tractor increased the pressure until one of his ribs cracked. He gasped for breath, desperate to get some air into his lungs, the tractor stopped for a second as if enjoying the pain Jim was in. Through the glare of the lights, he could see a black horned figure with piercing red eyes looking at him in the cab, and then he heard somebody whisper. "Die, die!" The tractor moved forward once more and Jim's ribcage was pushed into his chest, puncturing his lungs. He gasped one more time, and then his whole body went limp. The tractor reversed back into the tractor shed allowing Jim's lifeless body to slump to the floor. The lights on the tractor dimmed, then went out. A few seconds later the massive diesel engine turned over one more time then stopped.

The next morning it was Alfie who found the crumpled body of Jim Cleveland slumped against the cowshed. When the police and ambulance arrived, the forensics team were not far behind. They cordoned off the area, took photos and dusted for fingerprints and eventually took the body away for examination. Detective Peter Newman led the investigation.

"What's going to happen now?" Alfie asked him.

"We are treating this as a murder investigation and will be interviewing you and all the other farmworkers when the incident vehicle gets here," said Detective Newman. "So stick around, I want to speak to you first." When Stuart McDonald arrived he was not very pleased that his farm labourers were being questioned and not working.

"Look, detective, couldn't my men go back to work, and then you can interview them afterwards?" Detective Newman had a hard time controlling his anger.

"Mr McDonald!" he began in a raised voice, "This is a murder investigation, on your farm and you are one of the main suspects. So don't tell me what I can or can't do. Your men may have to take the day off, because nothing is going to be moved on this farm until I have completed the investigation. Is that clear?"

"Quite clear," replied Stuart McDonald, feeling a little humiliated. Then he turned and walked away, mumbling under his breath. After all the interviews had been completed it was late into the afternoon before the police moved off the farm, much to the delight of Stuart McDonald.

"Right lads, you can get back to work now, there are still a few hours of daylight left!" he bellowed. Alfie got into his cab, the engine roared into life and he drove off down the lane. When he was in the field and away from everybody he said: "John did you kill that man?" Again he had to wait for an answer as if the tractor was thinking the question through.

"He was going to harm me, so I eliminated him," replied the sinister voice.

Alfie didn't ask any more questions, he kept his thoughts to himself. When he had parked the tractor up for the night, John's soft voice had returned. He climbed down the ladder, and looked back at the menacing beast shimmering in the moonlight. What was dwelling in the depths of the tractor? A worrying thought crossed his mind: had the tractor been possessed by some evil spirit that could control the tractor any time it wanted to? Was he safe? What if the tractor turned on him? Who or what had taken over the JOHN DEERE? With these worrying thoughts turning over in his mind, he made his way back home.

CHAPTER 5

Alfie didn't tell anybody about what had happened. But a few days later Detective Newman was waiting for him when he arrived home.

"Alfred Bates, I would like you to accompany me down to the police station for further questioning. You have the right to remain silent but anything you do say may be given in evidence, do you understand?" Alfie was shaking, he held out his hand to his wife.

"Can I bring my family?" Alfie asked quietly. Detective Newman could see Alfie was frightened and relaxed his tone of voice.

"I'd rather you came alone, sir, I'm sure you won't be very long," replied the detective. Reluctantly Alfie was escorted to the waiting police car. He peered out of the rear window and watched his wife and children waving as he was driven off. Alfie was the main murder suspect. He was the only one who could drive the tractor, he was the only one the tractor was programmed to obey. He had two things in his favour, however. One: he had no motive, sure he knew Jim Cleveland, he had even offered Alfie a job, and he respected the man. And two: Alfie also had a perfect alibi: he was at his own birthday party among dozens of his friends. So two hours later Alfie returned home, much to the relief of his wife and family.

The murder baffled Detective Newman. One month later he was still no closer to solving the mystery, so the case was left open but unsolved.

Alfie still didn't tell anyone about the tractor, or the sinister voice. Who would believe him anyway? They would probably think he was insane. No, the best thing was to keep quiet; at least for the time being. Anyway Alfie had grown quite attached to his massive green friend, and it hadn't harmed him.

A week later, Stuart McDonald called Alfie into his office. He was sitting in his big leather reclining chair when Alfie walked in.

"I have been offered another new tractor" Stuart began. "It's the same model as before the 9639 T EXP, but this is the mark 2, it's been updated and improved. They've agreed to take the other tractor in exchange."

"You can't do that!" Alfie cried. "John's done everything I have asked it to, it's never let you down and does more than twice as much work as any other tractor in the area. Why get rid of it?"

"John?" Stuart chuckled, "are you calling my tractor, John?" Alfie felt a bit embarrassed. "Just remember who you are talking to young man, there are plenty of other men out there that would kill for your job. Anyway, I have already accepted the deal, the new tractor arrives at the end of the month, so say goodbye to John for me," he smirked. "Now get back to work!" Alfie trudged out of the office, he felt totally humiliated by Stuart McDonald, but he was right; there were plenty of other men looking for work. He pressed the remote key fob, climbed the ladder of the tractor and sank into his comfortable seat.

"Start your engine John," he heard himself say, his mind was on the thought of losing his beloved tractor. The engine burst into life, which awoke Alfie from his thoughts.

"Good morning, Alfie," came the familiar greeting, followed by: "What are we doing today?"

"We are fertilizing the top field" replied Alfie, "so hitch up the muck spreader" After they had collected the spreader they drove around to the huge pile of cow manure. Dave, the other farm hand loaded the spreader with the little Massey Fergusson's front bucket. And then Alfie set of along the lane to the top field. It was about two miles to the field, so Alfie pushed his foot hard down on the accelerator. The JOHN DEERE 9639 T EXP was quite capable of reaching 40 mph even on this bumpy terrain. After four loads Alfie pulled over for a quick drink from his flask.

"You are very quiet this morning," said John. "What is wrong?"

Alfie explained the situation, how his greedy boss had accepted a deal to exchange him for a more advanced tractor in three weeks' time.

"Am I not doing a good job?" asked John after Alfie had told him how Stuart McDonald had humiliated him.

"Of course you are!" replied Alfie. "No tractor works harder than you. It's just about my boss making even more money out of this deal, regardless of who he hurts." The tractor was silent for a few minutes. Alfie knew John was thinking things through. Suddenly the sinister voice spoke:

"I will deal with the problem in my own way."

Alfie didn't like the sound of this, so he decided not to question the voice further. He didn't want to know how the tractor would deal with the situation, but he had a good idea.

CHAPTER 6

It was a week later when Stuart McDonald was woken from a deep sleep by the sound of a revving tractor engine. He switched on the table light and looked at his watch. It was two am: "Who in God's name is driving a tractor at this time in the morning?" he thought to himself. His long suffering wife was still sound asleep, dreaming of a new life free from her husband's demands. Stuart quickly got dressed and went downstairs into the kitchen. He unlocked the gun cabinet, took out his twelve bore shotgun and loaded it with two cartridges.

"Nobody's going to drive off with one of my tractors and get away with it!" he said to himself. He grabbed a torch in his other hand and crept out over to the tractor shed. He could hear the engine being revved hard. He rounded the corner with the gun to his shoulder; the torch illuminating the side of the big green tractor. The engine immediately stopped.

"Come on out where I can see you!" he shouted. "I have a gun pointed straight at you, so come on out and show yourself!" An eerie silence drifted through the tractor shed. It was dark, but Stuart thought he saw a movement in the cab of the JOHN DEERE. He moved around to the front of the tractor and shone the torch into the cab.

Suddenly all the tractor's front lights switched on He couldn't see, so he squeezed the trigger on both barrels. The recoil from the shotgun sent him flying backwards and, before he could get up, the tractor was upon him, trapping his legs under the massive tracks. He tried to wriggle free as the twenty five ton beast slowly crawled up his legs. Then it stopped just above his knees. The pain was immense and he knew both his legs were broken. He screamed for help, but his cries were drowned out by the throb of the big diesel engine. Why had it stopped? Who was at the controls? In his imagination the engine seemed to slow into a loud throbbing heartbeat. Then the massive beast began to move forward again. It stopped again, just below his waist. Stuart had never endured this much pain. He started to pass out. Why hadn't it just run over him and put him out of his misery? The last thing Stuart saw was the front of the tractor which seemed to be grinning as it slowly ran over him, crushing his body into the soft mud.

Alfie arrived early the next morning as he had a lot of work to get through and wanted to get a good start. Nobody was around when he made his way over to the tractor shed. He stopped short when he spotted the big green tractor parked just outside the tractor shed. Hadn't he parked the tractor inside the shed the night before? Alfie moved slowly around the tractor looking for anything suspicious, but everything seemed normal. Maybe he had miscalculated the position of the tractor. It was very dark when he had parked and he was extremely tired. In his mind he had accepted the explanation, and then he pressed the remote and climbed the ladder into the cab. He was greeted with the usual. "Good morning, Alfie" when he instructed John to start the engine. Then the sinister voice interrupted: "I have dealt with our problem."

"What problem?" Alfie asked.

"I won't have to be exchanged," replied the voice.

"What have you done?" asked Alfie. There was no answer for some time. Alfie was just about to ask again when the voice replied.

"When there is an obstacle in the way, I eliminate it." Alfie didn't want to know what obstacle John was talking about, but he had a gut feeling something dreadful had happened. He instructed the tractor to move forward as he took the controls. He glanced behind him as the tractor moved off, there in the track marks lay the crushed body of Stuart McDonald. Alfie stopped the tractor. Panic gripped him; he knew he wouldn't get away with it this time.

Who would believe him? He had no alibi and everybody knew he hated his boss. He would be convicted and go to prison for the rest of his life. His wife and children would be homeless and destitute. He couldn't let this happen. Alfie climbed down the ladder and went over to the mangled body; he then looked at his watch. It was still early, Dave didn't start till seven thirty and Mrs McDonald didn't get up until eight. He had a least half an hour to get rid of the body, but where? Then he had the answer.

Several years ago the farm kept pigs until the boss found it was unprofitable and he sold them all off. The big silage pit was still there, covered with a large concrete slab to stop anybody falling in He quickly drove the tractor around to the pit, tied a chain around the concrete slab and pulled it off, just enough so he could get a body through the gap. He looked at his watch; he still had twenty minutes. Alfie didn't like the thought of picking the body up so he drove the old Massey Ferguson tractor with the front bucket attached and scooped the crushed body into the bucket. All he had to do now was to push the body through the gap into the pit below He heard the body splash into the pigs' waste material. It stank so much it made Alfie heave, but he knew the pit was at least twenty feet deep and the body would dissolve in the toxic waste material.

He quickly pushed the heavy concrete slab back into its original position, using the old tractor's front bucket. It struggled moving the two tons of heavy concrete back into place. He then sprinkled dust over the area and was finally satisfied the slab looked as though it had never been moved. He drove the old tractor back to the shed and parked it up. Then Alfie checked the ground where the body had been, to make sure everything had been picked up. He spotted the shotgun partly buried in the mud.

He picked it up then glanced at his watch again; he had no time to throw the shotgun down the pit, Dave would be here soon, so he put it behind the seat of the JOHN DEERE and then he drove the tractor over the area several times, eliminating any trace of evidence. When this had been done Alfie connected the harrows to the JOHN DEERE and set off down the field. He was relieved he had resolved the situation. Alfie spotted Dave away in the distance pedalling his bike as fast as he could, he waved but Dave was too busy concentrating on getting to work on time. He didn't want his boss docking his wages again.

CHAPTER 7

Jean McDonald got up as usual at ten past eight; she looked across at her husband's empty bed, and wasn't surprised to see he had already got up. He did this quite often just to check on what time his men arrived at work. But when he didn't come home for his usual ten o' clock fried breakfast, Jean became worried. She slipped the meal under the grill to keep warm, put on her wellies and went over to the tractor shed.

"Have you seen Stuart this morning?" she asked Dave who was repairing the punctured tyre on the muck spreader

"No, Mrs McDonald. I have been her since seven thirty, but I haven't seen Stuart." He paused, "Maybe he went out with Alfie, I saw him driving towards the long meadow this morning." Jean thanked Dave and went back into the house.

"Well, if he wants a dried up breakfast then that's what he'll get," she muttered under her breath as she washed up the dirty saucepans. It wasn't until Alfie returned in the afternoon and told Jean he had not seen her husband, that Mrs McDonald phoned the police and reported her husband missing. After Inspector Newman had taken her statement and had talked to Alfie and Dave, she was assured that the police would circulate a description of her husband and keep her informed if they had any more information. As there were no suspicious circumstances, the police filed the case under missing persons. But there was still no sign of him a month later.

Alfie had persuaded Mrs McDonald to cancel the order for the new tractor, which was quite easy really because she had a soft spot for Alfie and hated the way her husband treated him. After twelve months Stuart McDonald had still not been found. The police reopened the case, with various television appeals for information, still nobody came forward with any news. So the police closed the investigation down.

It was the start of the harvest when Mrs McDonald broke the news to Alfie and Dave that she was selling the farm. She spoke to both men separately. Alfie walked into the main house, knocked on the office door, and was invited in by the smartly dressed Mrs McDonald. Alfie sat down nervously, dreading the expected news of his redundancy.

"Alfie" Mrs McDonald began "You have worked here for how many years?"

"Ten years, Ma'am," Alfie replied.

"And how many times has Mr McDonald paid you a bonus?" she asked. Alfie didn't have to think very hard about that question.

"None Ma'am, I don't think he has ever paid anybody a bonus." was his reply.

"I thought so" replied Mrs McDonald. "Well, I am giving you both a bonus for all the hard work you have done over the years."

Alfie didn't expect to hear this and asked "What's going to happen to the JOHN DEERE, Ma'am?"

"You like that tractor, don't you Alfie?" she paused. "Well, how would you like to own it?" Alfie couldn't believe his ears.

"Own it, Ma'am? What do you mean? I can't afford to buy it."

"You don't have to buy it, Alfie. I am giving you the tractor and all the equipment that comes with it, as the bonus."

Alfie sat silently for a few minutes; he could feel the tears welling up. Nobody had given him anything in his life. With tears running down his face he replied "Thank you ma'am, that's very generous of you." He got up and shook Mrs

McDonald's hand. He couldn't wait to get out of the office and tell his wife.

Mrs McDonald kept her word and handed over the legal documents for the tractor the next day. She also gave Dave a cheque for thirty thousand pounds for the three years that he had been working on the farm. And that wasn't the only surprise that Mrs McDonald had arranged. When Mr and Mrs Brown the new owners moved in, they offered Alfie and Dave a job on a self-employed basis, meaning Alfie could hire himself and his tractor out to anybody willing to pay a decent wage. He immediately unscrewed the advertising board on the front of the tractor, and then replaced it a few days later.

It read: TO HIRE ME phone ALFIE on 07850 394502. He stood back and surveyed his handy work. Alfie felt very proud of the JOHN DEERE, he cleaned and polished it every Sunday; he didn't want to be seen driving a dirty tractor. Alfie worked out a rota: he worked three days a week for the Browns; two days a week for Mrs Cleveland at the large farm on the other side of the valley; and one day a week for a small farm about a mile away. The money just kept coming in; he had never been so well off.

But there was a bad side to Alfie, he had changed or the JOHN DEERE had changed him. He had a terrible attitude and was becoming greedy and conceited, only working for the highest payer. His wife and kids hardly saw their father as he was spending more and more time with the tractor. One night, on the rare occasion they were in bed, together, Alfie's wife noticed the changes and it frightened her. Dark lines ran down his face making it look drawn and haggard. His once bright eyes were now black sunken holes peering at her with hatred. She pushed him away as he tried to kiss her, his breath smelt like rotten meat. She got out of bed went downstairs and slept in the spare bedroom.

CHAPTER 8

It was the last week in August and very hot. Alfie was ploughing the top field for Mr Brown. He had been driving the tractor very hard for over eight hours. It was getting late; the last traces of daylight were fading fast, so he drove the tractor even harder. Small whiffs of smoke started drifting up from the floor. Alfie stopped the engine. At first he couldn't see where the smoke was coming from; he switched on the lights in the cab and then realized the circuit boards under his seat were on fire. He tried to unlatch the fire extinguisher at the side of the seat and burnt his hand in the process.

He cried out "John, help me!" but there was no answer. When he tried to get up the arm rests seemed to close in on him even more, trapping him in the seat. He kicked out at the controls. The toxic smoke from the seat now filled the cab. Alfie screamed as the skin on his buttocks and tops of his legs began to burn and his once comfy seat seemed to grip him even tighter.

He wriggled and struggled even more. He then pushed down on the arm rests with all his strength and managed to free himself from the seat. Gasping for breath he tried to open the cab door, but it was locked. Alfie screamed "Unlock the door, John!" Seconds later the sinister voice replied. "If I die, then you will die." Alfie suddenly remembered the hammer in the toolbox; he knew he only had minutes before he was overcome by the smoke and fumes. With hands that felt on fire he pulled out the tool box and opened the lid. He couldn't see, his eyes were swollen with the smoke. He started to cough violently, he fumbled around until his hand gripped the hammer. With his last remaining strength he struck the glass back window with the hammer. It didn't break so he tried again: the glass remained intact.

He suddenly remembered the escape hatch in the roof Paul had told him about. He reached up and felt for the catch through the smoke, his breathing was becoming shallow and his throat seemed on fire. At last his fingers found the catch and twisted it. The hatch swung open. He stood on the burning seat and pushed his head and shoulders through the small opening, gasping for air. He pushed down on the hot cab roof with scalding hands and tried to lift himself clear. Something was holding on to his burning legs with a vice like grip. He kicked and thrashed about with his legs until he was free.

He pulled himself out of the cab and then slammed the trapdoor shut. He slid down the front of the tractor onto the tracks and then fell on the ground.

He lay there gasping for breath until he had enough strength to crawl away from the burning machine. Alfie was in agony, his legs were raw, and his hands were so badly burnt he couldn't see his fingers. His face and throat were badly swollen from the toxic fumes he had inhaled. He managed to pull himself up to a sitting position and look at the burning tractor. He was at least ten feet from the machine, but could still feel the intense heat. A wailing scream could be heard over the roaring fire. Through the smoke and fire Alfie could just make out a horned face in the flames, its horrid tortured features swathed in agony as it burnt. Was this the evil demon that had possessed his beloved tractor? Alfie sat mesmerized. He couldn't take his eyes off the horned demon.

A distorted voice suddenly screamed "Help me!" But Alfie couldn't move and the pain from his burnt body became so unbearable he passed out. Alfie lay in the field all night, it was early morning before he regained conciseness, and the pain hit him like a sledgehammer. His body was so stiff it felt as if it was glued into the soil. He looked across at the burnt out shell of the JOHN DEERE tractor. A few whiffs of smoke still drifted up into the morning sunshine, but there was no sign of the hideous demon. It was midday before a farm worker spotted the burnt out tractor and came over to investigate, and it was another hour before the ambulance rushed Alfie to the hospital.

When he awoke the next morning he was in a hospital bed, and bandages covered over fifty per cent of his body. His wife and children were all at his bedside and were relieved when he looked at them and smiled. Alfie was in hospital for three months. Two of his fingers had to be amputated and his legs were badly scarred, although he could still walk. The fire had not burnt his face, but the toxic smoke had affected his breathing. Despite this, he felt as if a weight had been taken from his shoulders. Two weeks after he arrived home he received a cheque from the insurance company for the burnt out tractor.

Development of the JOHN DEERE 9639 T EXP model was shelved two weeks later, due to escalating costs. Alfie managed to buy one of the last JOHN DEERE 9639 T models. His wife saw a change in her husband over the next months; he was much more caring and thoughtful.

Alfie only drove the tractor for five days a week, and then spent the weekends with his family. But he was always the happiest when he sat behind the wheel of the JOHN DEERE 9639 T, the strongest and most advanced tractor in the world.

HO 229 V6

PART 1

Erwin Ziller was a test pilot during the 2nd World War. As one of an elite group, he became the chief test pilot for the Horton HO 229, Hitler's experimental plane. The Gothaer Waggonfabrik Company built the plane just outside the city of Gotha and its existence was a closely guarded secret. On February 18th 1945 Erwin Ziller planned to fly the latest version of the plane, the HO 229 V6. It was a cloudy evening, not ideal conditions for testing the fastest and most advanced fighter bomber in the world. On this particular flight it had been fitted out with the most up to date secret weaponry Germany had ever designed. Erwin knew this was Hitler's last chance to gain control of the skies. If this plane failed to live up to his expectations then the war was lost, and Erwin was determined not to let down the Fuhrer.

He attached the special Perspex helmet onto his suit, secured the lid of the cockpit, and started to taxi down the runway. He thrust the controls forward and let the Jumo jet engines reach full throttle before ascending into the cloudy sky. As this was an experimental flight he put the plane through a series of hoops and rolls. He then took the plane up to 50,000 feet but hit some turbulent weather. So he decided to climb even higher to get above the bad weather. He levelled out at 60,000 feet, the highest the plane had ever been flown. The air was thin at this height, so Erwin opened the twin jet engines even more and watched the speed increase to 700 mph. Suddenly the plane began to shudder and vibrate, but he gripped the controls even harder and did not throttle back. Erwin knew he was approaching the speed of sound.

What would it be like to be the first person to break through the sound barrier? The Fuhrer would be so proud of him. Erwin flew straight and level, even though the plane was buffeting the speed kept increasing: 710, 720. Just as Erwin thought he had pushed the plane far enough there was a loud bang. The buffeting stopped and the plane's controls eased off. Erwin looked at his speed: 738 mph—he had passed through the sound barrier. A big smile spread across his face. No other plane could get anywhere near that speed.

But his smile soon vanished when he noticed some of the dials were not working. His altimeter was stuck on 50,000 feet; he flicked it with his finger but the gauge didn't move. He tried to make contact with the ground, but the radio was dead. He looked at the other gauges; the only ones that seemed to be working were the fuel tanks and they both registered over half full. Erwin was flying blind; he didn't know his height, he didn't know which direction he was flying and worst of all, he didn't know where he was. He eased back on the controls and let the plane descend gradually.

At 40,000 feet he was still in the clouds and it was getting darker. He looked at his watch and realized he had been flying for over an hour. Erwin dropped down even lower: 30,000 feet then 20,000 feet, but he was still in black clouds. He calculated he was flying west by north-west. If he turned the plane around in a long sweep and headed south by south-east he should arrive back where he started He noticed the fuel gauges hadn't altered. He flicked them with his finger, and realized they were not working ether.

Panic began to grip him; he would have to fly even lower and break out of the clouds, then land at the nearest runway. Erwin checked his radio again, but it was dead. Nothing seemed to be working. He dropped down to 10,000 feet and levelled out; at least he was below cloud level and could see lights on the ground. But he still hadn't a clue as to where he was. Erwin tried to look for familiar land marks: rivers, tall buildings, railway lines, but he did not recognize anything.

Suddenly one engine spluttered then cut out. He wrestled with the controls and managed to keep control, and then the other engine cut out without any warning. Erwin knew his fuel tanks were empty. He kept the plane parallel with the ground as he lowered the landing wheels and hoped there was a flat piece of land ahead. The plane dropped rapidly out of the sky. It hit a small hill and broke into several pieces. The fuselage was catapulted into the air then nose-dived into the ground. Erwin Ziller was killed instantly when his head hit the canopy.

PART 2

In 2013 Jonathan Palmer moved to Dublin after living in Wales for most of his life. He was an aeronautical relic hunter to give him his proper title, which meant he dug up old aeroplanes to see what he could salvage and then sold the parts to collectors or museums. It wasn't his full time job, he was a self-employed builder, but at weekends and holidays Jon was happiest when he was digging holes in the ground looking for crashed WW11 aeroplanes. He didn't work alone. There were four other men who were just as keen to unearth hidden treasures:

Tom Wilkenshore owned a small plane which he used to fly the team over the land to see if there were any imperfections in the ground. Sometimes you could see the outline of objects buried beneath the soil, especially if the weather had been dry for several weeks.

Ben Fletcher owned and operated his own excavator, which made it a whole lot easier if the wreckage was deep. If he could get to the site then Ben could dig it up. Shaun Murphy held an HGV driving licence and owned a small transport business, but he also owned an articulated lorry which was big enough to carry Ben's excavator to and from sites.

Andy Butcher was an historian, but his specialist subject was WW11 aviation. He knew the history of any plane, whether Russian, German, French or any other European or American aircraft. If it flew then Andy knew its history.

So the five men made a formidable team and had already unearthed some valuable items.

Jonathan was the team leader and often went along to the Royal Air Force Museum where they kept a record of all the missing aircraft that either crashed or were shot down over Great Britain during the war. They even kept records of the approximate locations of the crash sites. If the plane looked interesting and had some historical value, Jonathan would apply to the MoD for permission to excavate the wreckage. This was sometimes refused if it was classified secret or of a sensitive nature.

While browsing through the thousands of records, Jonathan noticed a Spitfire had crashed into the Bog of Allen in central Ireland. He was particularly interested as this was one of the largest peat bogs in Ireland and, because peat bogs were soft, the planes suffered less damage and were better preserved. The downside was the sites were difficult to get to and very often the wreckage was buried quite deep, as the peat was up to 10 metres deep in places. But this Spitfire had crashed in February 1945 and was one of the last made. He wrote off to the MoD for permission to excavate the wreckage. Two weeks later he received a letter giving them permission to excavate. Jon phoned around all his friends and they agreed to start work on the project two weeks later.

The whole team arrived on site on August 2nd as planned. The crash site was on the outskirts of the bog, about half a mile from Croghan Hill. Shaun had brought some duckboards along just in case the ground was wet and to give support for the 5 ton excavator. They set up camp on a high spot halfway up Croghan Hill overlooking the crash site. The plan was to dig a series of pilot holes in a half mile radius to see if they could find any part of the wreckage.

In some cases the wreckage could be spread over a mile so it was like looking for a needle in a haystack. If they could find and identify any part of the plane then the team knew they were in the right area. Because the Spitfire was mostly made of wood, the wings were not normally very deep, perhaps a metre down. The fuselage would be a bit deeper, but the engine, the only really solid part of the plane, could be as much as two to three metres deep.

They began digging the pilot holes at midday. By nightfall nothing had been found, not even a nut or bolt. After cooking up some burgers and hotdogs on the gas barbeque, they decided to turn in and make an early start the next morning. At 7.30 am after a very early breakfast, Ben started up the Volvo excavator and began digging another series of holes.

"Go down a little deeper this time" said Jonathan "The ground is quite soft here." In the second hole they found part of a propeller and Andy identified it as belonging to a Spitfire.

"We have to find part of the fuselage or engine" said Andy, "Something with serial numbers on to see if it's the same plane."

They continued digging and uncovered a piece of shiny metal. Ben switched off the engine then jumped in the hole. He shouted to the others.

"I've found something, get some shovels!" Jon passed Ben a shovel and he began digging. He dug carefully, not wanting to damage the shiny metal.

"What is it?" asked Jon.

"Well it's definitely not from a Spitfire," said Ben. "It's aluminium." They all jumped into the trench to touch the shiny metal.

"Come on" said Andy, "Let's get this exposed before nightfall and identify it." By four o'clock they still hadn't unearthed the shiny structure. In all the years Andy had been researching warplanes he had never seen anything like this before and he was becoming very excited.

"Do you think it could be some type of alien spacecraft?" he said suddenly. The other men stopped digging and looked at him in amusement.

"Good God, Andy!" replied Shaun. "You'll be telling us next to watch out for little green men!" They all burst out laughing, including Andy.

"Yes I suppose it was a stupid idea," said Andy. "If only we could find some markings or serial numbers then they might give us a clue as to where it came from"

Ben suggested looping several canvas straps under the object and lifting it with the excavator arm. He got back in the excavator and lowered the arm over the object so the men could attach the straps. Then he slowly began to lift; the object was quite flexible and began to twist. There was a loud ripping of metal and it suddenly broke free and was dangling above the ground.

The men stared at it in disbelief. It looked like part of a wing but it was triangular shaped. Ben lowered it on to a flat piece of ground so they could all get a closer look It was only about 6 inches thick at the wing tip, thickening to about two feet at the widest end, which was at least eight feet across. But this was hard to establish, as a lot of the wing was missing. Andy examined it more closely; he took off his gloves and ran his hand over the smooth, shiny surface. He was amazed at the condition of the metal. There was no rust or decay of any kind and hardly any indentations which Andy found hard to believe, because whatever it was it had definitely crash-landed. At the widest part he could see something had been attached to it, an engine maybe or part of the landing gear, but he was only guessing which he found very frustrating.

"Let's dig a bit deeper" said Andy. "We may find an engine or something to establish where it came from and what it was" He felt a little embarrassed at not being able to identify the object for certain, as he was meant to be the expert. But the men resumed digging and by early afternoon had found what looked like a jet engine. Shaun put the straps around the engine and gently lifted it clear of the excavation. It wasn't in as good condition as the wing part.

Mud had been rammed into the air intake when it hit the ground and some of the casing had been ripped off on impact. Andy and Jon eagerly started cleaning the mud out of the engine. Ten minutes later he let out a yell. "I've found something lads!"

He took a cloth and rubbed at the engraved lettering on the inside of the cowling. It read Jumo 004C. He quickly washed his hands and ran over to his car. There he sorted through some of the specialist books he carried on jet engines. By then the other men had joined him.

"Come on then," said Shaun. "What can you tell us?" Andy didn't reply for a few seconds as he was still reading a page from one of his books.

"Well, it's definitely German" said Andy. "The engine was made by Junkers, a German company, but I can't see anything about the Jumo 004C engine. It must be a later development of the Axial Turbo Jet 004B" He turned around and showed them the picture of the HORTON HO229B.

"This, gentlemen, is what we have uncovered: Hitler's secret plane, the most advanced plane of the 2nd World War, but the war finished before they could be produced and very few actually flew. This must be one of the last ever made. America has the only other intact example of this plane, anywhere in the world. If we could find the rest of the plane" he paused and took a deep breath. "Then it could be worth a fortune." All the men let out a cheer.

"Come on" said Shaun excitedly. "Let's drink to that!" He went to his tent and came back with 5 bottles of beer. They drank the beer and celebrated. Jon looked down over the crash site and then glanced up to the top of the hill.

"The pilot must have come down and hit the top of the hill there." Pointing to a ridge running along the top he continued "The wings must have been ripped off on impact, and the fuselage would have been catapulted over in that direction." He pointed over to an area at least hundred yards from the crash site. The men looked at each other in disappointment. They all knew they faced a mammoth task of finding the fuselage and then recovering it. They drank another beer and then retired for the night.

Jon was up bright and early the next day. He began pacing up and down the hill, and then wrote in his notebook. He then went back up the hill with a sighting rod and a parallax rangefinder, a small instrument that calculates distances. He estimated that if the plane crashed with the landing wheels down, it might have been flying at less than 200 mph, hit the ridge and nosedived into the bog approximately 98 yards from the point of impact. Of course this was all theory. They hadn't found any landing gear, the plane might have nosedived straight in to the bog, but Jon thought this unlikely as they had only found part of the wing and engine. So his theory was all they had to go on. He showed the men his drawing and calculations when they were having breakfast.

"I suppose I could dig a long trench to your measurements" said Ben "It may take longer but would cover a wider area."

They all thought this a good idea. Ben began excavating, while the others carried on digging out the other holes by hand. Jon was having a cigarette wondering whether he had made the right calculations when Tom suddenly stood up and shouted "I think I've found something!" They all went over to the hole that Tom had been digging. Sure enough, Tom had unearthed part of the engine.

"I think it's still attached to the wing" said Tom excitedly. This time they knew what shape the wing would be, so

Ben tracked back along the duckboards to where Tom had uncovered the engine and began digging. He only removed the top layer of soil, letting the others remove the remaining soil so as not to damage their valuable find. Within an hour they had uncovered the entire wing with the engine still attached.

"That's amazing!" said Tom, standing back to admire his find. "It's hardly damaged, this plane must have been incredibly strong to survive the impact" The others agreed, but Jon was not among them. He'd disappeared back to his car to fetch his note book.

The others looked on as he scrambled back up the hill with his sighting rod. A few minutes later, he began waving his arms and pointing in a westerly direction. They didn't know what he was trying to tell them, so waited until the breathless Jonathan joined them. It took him several minutes before he had recovered enough to speak.

"We are digging in the wrong place," he said, still wheezing a bit. "We should be digging over there." He pointed to the right of the trench Ben had started. "Look, I've done some more calculations, based on the position of the wings. I now think the plane hit the ridge at an angle. The left hand wing ploughed into the ground first, ripping off the wheel and wing. It then bounced back in the air turning slightly to the right. It then nosedived into the ground ripping the other wing and engine off."

Jon looked at his notes again and began pacing steps from the second wing. He stopped about 30 feet away. "I think the fuselage is buried right under my feet" he said. He pushed a marker into the ground to mark the spot. The men looked at each other; you could see the excitement in their faces.

"Let's get digging!" said Ben eagerly.

"Just a minute" said Jon "Let's see if we can find the other parts of the plane first before we go making any more holes, it already looks like a bomb site" The others agreed as they were all feeling a bit tired and hungry.

It was a bit easier to calculate where the rest of the plane was. They found the other part of the wing still attached to the engine a little deeper and about 6 feet further to the north. Then Shaun found one wheel and then the other, not far away from the wings, but again a bit deeper. Now that they had found most of the plane's wings and undercarriage, the men decided to head off to the nearest pub for a bite to eat and a pint of liquid nectar. Jon told his men to keep quiet about what they had found.

"We don't want half of Ireland descending on our site looking for souvenirs" he said as they made their way to the pub. At 11.30pm five men returned to the camp a little worse for wear.

They all tucked into their sleeping bags and were soon fast asleep, except for Jon. He was thinking, had he got his calculations right? They had been lucky so far. If only they could find the missing fuselage intact, he then slowly drifted off into a deep sleep.

Ben was the first to get up and began waking all the others. Jon was still sound asleep when Ben shook him.

"Come on mate!" said Ben. "Its 7.30 and we've got a plane to find." Jon wearily made his way over to the makeshift table the others had erected. Shaun had already made breakfast, so Jon sat down and started to eat.

"I'm going to make a start," said Ben and walked over to his excavator. The others followed. Ben started filling in the holes, while the others looked out for any small objects they had missed. By mid-morning the excavation site had been levelled. Shaun had found a few small items, but nothing of significance and the strange thing was they had not found any more of the Spitfire which surprised Jon because they usually found ammunition of some sort and the Spitfire's engine always survived. But he guessed they had just not dug deep enough, or were in the wrong place.

Now all their focus was on the new dig. Ben positioned his excavator over the marker stick and began digging. The others had to just wait, they all knew they would have to stop soon and get back to their real jobs so it was imperative they found the fuselage today. By midday Ben had dug a deep trench but had not found anything except an old tin helmet, which was in poor condition and worthless.

"Try digging another trench to the right of this one!" Jon shouted to Ben. He filled in part of the trench and began digging another. Ben had only scraped down about two feet when Andy shouted "Stop!" He jumped down into the trench and looked closely at the soil. He pointed at a sharp piece of metal just poking out of the ground.

"Ben, you have just taken the very tip of the tail from the fuselage" Andy said triumphantly. The men jumped into the trench and began exposing the end section of the fuselage. Ben changed the bucket on his digger for a smaller one so he could dig down the side of the frame more accurately.

One hour later they had uncovered half of the fuselage. Jon could see it had nosedived into the ground at an angle. The ground around the plane was getting extremely soft as they dug deeper. Another hour later they had to support the body of the plane to keep it from buckling. At 8ft deep Ben could no longer use the excavator as it was becoming extremely dangerous working so close to the body and as the ground was so soft, there was a possibility the excavator might topple into the trench. Ben backed off the excavator and sat on some firmer ground. He then set the arm of the excavator over the plane, and fastened the straps around the fuselage to support the weight when the plane finally broke free. Only the glass cockpit canopy and the front of the plane were now still buried in the soft peat. Digging by hand was a lot harder especially at 8ft deep. But Ben had dug a big enough hole for the men to work in so it wasn't too bad, just tiring.

Andy was uncovering the cockpit and was surprised to see the glass was still intact after the impact; he wiped the glass with his sleeve.

"Oh my God!" he cried. "The pilot is still in there!" They all crowded around to get a better look. Erwin Ziller's body was still strapped inside the airtight cockpit. His body had been miraculously preserved by the peat bog.

"We must inform the police and the MoD" said Andy. "They will know what to do." None of them had ever uncovered a body before, so the authorities would probably take over the operation as soon as they were informed.

"Let's call them tomorrow," said Shaun. "At least then we can get the fuselage out in one piece. It will still be valuable and we get the credit for finding it." They all agreed and began the final dig to free the plane from its soggy grave. By late afternoon the fuselage was laying on a flat piece of ground fully exposed. Andy covered the cockpit glass canopy with a blanket. He thought it only right to cover the body.

That final night in their tents, all the men were very happy knowing that they may have found a valuable piece of WW11 history. The next morning Jon phoned the MoD and let them take over the operation. Within the hour army trucks and cranes descended on the Bog of Allen and sealed off the area. They lifted the fuselage on to an articulated low loader and covered it with sheeting. Another lorry took away the wings and undercarriage. By now the press and TV had heard about the mysterious find on the peat bog, and wanted to know what had been found. But the lieutenant in charge of the operation didn't give any press releases, and they were escorted off the site by the army.

Andy received a letter from the MoD congratulating the team on the professional way they had handled the situation and advising they would be formally rewarded once the body had been removed and the relations had been informed. And they were all invited back to see the plane after the engineers had pieced it back together.

PART 3

Lieutenant George Banner had been put in charge of Operation Horton. The plane had been brought to a hangar at RAF Brize Norton where a specialist team of aircraft engineers planned to restore the plane to its original condition. The RAF was particularly interested in the plane. They knew Hitler had been building a futuristic plane, but had never seen one in the flesh, only in photographs. The plane was far more advanced than anything Britain or America had in the war.

The first job was to extract the body of the pilot. However, when the aircraft engineer assigned to remove the body peered into the cockpit he noticed a bomb-like warhead had pierced the bulkhead and had pushed the pilot's seat forward. He quickly raised the alarm and the hangar was evacuated until the bomb squad arrived.

It wasn't long before the familiar green lorries drove into the hangar. Sergeant Ben Ashford was the leader of the elite four man team. Ben soon realised they couldn't extract the object through the cockpit; they would have to open the cargo bay doors on the underside of the plane. As the fuselage had already been raised up on a small scaffold, the men could see the underside of the plane. There was no visible release catch to the cargo bay doors, so Ben decided to force the doors open with a jemmy bar. At first they didn't seem to budge, but with two men pulling on the bars they suddenly dropped open.

Nobody noticed an odourless gas now seeping from the once airtight cargo hold.

Ben quickly assessed the situation. There were three cylindrical canisters held in a metal rack. Each was about 6ft long and about 2ft in diameter, with what looked like a pointed warhead or detonating cap at the front. The middle one had broken free and pierced the airtight bulkhead on the pilot's cabin. There was no room inside the cargo hold for them to disconnect the detonators.

The only way to release the bombs was to cut the mangled rack holding them in place. Ben thought it might be risky using an electric disc cutter because of the sparks, so decided to do it the old fashioned way, using a hacksaw. It was a slow task, but they eventually managed to lower the live bombs, one by one, to the ground. Ben thought they did not look like conventional bombs. They had a nosecone, but the main body was shaped like a crude 40 gallon oil drum.

Suddenly Ben began to feel unwell and fell to the floor. He began to hallucinate, and imagined he was being threatened. The other men, thinking he was having a fit, quickly covered him with a blanket and called an ambulance. Ben seemed to recover quickly and stood up. He looked around with a blank expression and without warning picked up a spanner and repeatedly hit one of his men across the head, before the rest of the team overpowered him. They held him down and disarmed him. Ben was kicking and flailing his arms around wildly, even though two men were sitting on him. He suddenly clutched his chest, took one last breath and was still.

The other men began violently attacking one another and by the time the ambulance arrived they were all dead. The two paramedics couldn't believe their eyes. What had been a routine callout for a man described as having a fit was now a war zone, with blood-covered bodies everywhere.

One by one the men were brought out and put in the ambulance. Then soldiers sealed off the hangar. Whatever it was that had killed the men, at least it could be contained in the airtight building. The ambulance then drove off to the mortuary where the bodies would be examined. But the ambulance never arrived at the mortuary. One of the paramedics attacked the other driver with a scalpel and the ambulance crashed, killing both paramedics.

Four of the Army personnel that had sealed the hangar also met grisly deaths before the situation was under control. Biological chemical weapons experts were called in to find out what had been released inside the hangar. Wearing the latest protective suits the two men entered the hangar. Then the door was sealed behind them again. Charles Brogan, the more experienced of the two, approached the canisters. They all looked intact, but after closer inspection he could see the middle canister that had broken free and penetrated the bulkhead had a very small crack at the front of the canister.

He took out a small instrument which registered any anomalies in the air, and held it over the damaged area. The needle moved slowly to critical: some sort of chemical pollutant was leaking into the air. Charles used a quick hardening solution to stop the leak. After this was done he checked all the other canisters, but did not discover any more leaks. However, the building was still contaminated.

Charles organized a decontamination crew that specialized in chemical releases. They pumped in a special gas that neutralizes dangerous chemicals. Within 24 hours the building was declared safe and the army dressed in their protective suits defused the detonation caps, then loaded the canisters into a lorry. They were later buried in an undisclosed waste facility.

Jonathan Palmer and his team were all invited back to see the Horton HO 229 flying wing assembled and marvelled at how the plane resembled the modern stealth fighter of today. Weeks later they were all rewarded by the MOD with a small contribution towards their costs, sadly not the big pay-out they had been expecting. The plane was destroyed in a fire two months later before it could be put on display to the public.

Scientists later analysed the deadly gas which caused such violent hallucinations and a horrible death. The scientists had never seen this type of gas before. Was Hitler planning to detonate the deadly bombs over Britain in a last minute ditch to beat the stubborn little island that he had failed to defeat? Only he knew the answer to that.

THE APPLE STORE

PART 1

I first met Reg in 1962 when I started school at Blackstone School in Wallingford. The school was about four miles from my house, so every morning the school bus picked me up on its rounds around the other villages. On the way to school we passed through Brightwell cum Sotwell, a pretty little village on the outskirts of Wallingford. Reg would be waiting under the old chestnut tree on the top road. When I first saw him I could see he came from a poor family as he was rather scruffily dressed in short trousers, at 11 years old he was the only boy wearing them.

All the other boys wore long trousers, so that was the start of the Mickey taking. I felt sorry for Reg, so when he walked down the bus to find a seat I let him sit next to me. We started talking and I found out his father also worked on a local farm as a tractor driver. Our backgrounds were similar and soon we became best friends. We met up with another boy from a nearby village; Shaun Williams was his name, a big muscley lad. Nobody picked a fight with him, so the three of us made a formidable trio. We went through school life like most young teenagers. As we became closer Reg would tell me about his home life. He had 2 brothers and 2 sisters, all younger than him. It was a struggle for his mother bringing up 5 children in a tied farm cottage, on just a farm labourer's wage. So that was why Reg was always dressed in second-hand clothes.

Discipline at home was strict and often ended in violence. His father was the main culprit, regularly beating him with a belt if he misbehaved. He often wondered why his father took no interest in him, and why he got the most beatings. He would run away and spend all day in the nearby woods, making tree camps, and sometimes spending the night in them. But his mother always knew where he was and would go and fetch him back. So Reg did not have a happy home life, and rather enjoyed going to school. Blackstone was a mixed school, so we all experienced falling in and out of love quite regularly. Reg was different though, he didn't have many girlfriends. But there was one girl he fell deeply in love with. Her name was Brenda Wiley and she lived on a caravan park at Shillingford Hill. Her mother who lived in London could not cope, so Brenda had been sent to stay with her Grandmother until things improved at home. I suppose Reg was about 14 years old then. He was always talking about her in class and often got told off, for gas bagging as some teachers put it. But it all came to an abrupt end when Brenda had to go back home to London.

Reg never quite got over it and moped about for a few months afterwards. When he left school he joined a local building firm, and did an apprenticeship in carpentry. Shaun and I were working on building sites, but after a couple of years we became bored with this and decided to go to Australia. Back then Australia was promoting the Assisted Passage Scheme. If you were a skilled tradesman, especially in the building trade, the Australian Government would pay for your passage by ship, on condition you stayed for at least 2 years. We tried to get Reg to join us, but he had fallen in love again with a local girl, and would not leave her. So we left for Australia in June 1970. I didn't see Reg again for 10 years.

We met up again when I came back. While we had been in Australia Reg had got married and had three children, so there was a lot of catching up to do. He had done well for himself after becoming a self-employed builder. He would buy a house, then build an extension or renovate it, live in it for a couple of years then sell it at a profit. It meant the family were always moving, but Reg would always say. "I have never won anything and nobody's going to give me anything. The only way I can become rich is to work bloody hard". And that is what he did, often working 7 days a week.

Later on when I joined the police force I moved away from the area and lost touch with Reg. It was on my 50th birthday that I received a phone call.

"Do you fancy coming out for a meal and a drink?"

I knew straight away it was Reg. So we met up at a local restaurant. Reg was a changed man, very generous and friendly. He paid for the meals, and from that day on his nickname was Reg the Wedge because he always carried a bundle of twenty pound notes. He now owned a villa in Spain, a 1 bedroom flat, a 2 bedroom semidetached house, and a large 4 bedroom detached house in 3 acres of ground. He told me he had a mortgage on most of the properties, but the rent easily paid these, and he had enough left over to live on. So things were going well for Reg.

That was probably the high point in his life. From then on it was all downhill. A year later his father died, which didn't seem to upset Reg much, but when his mother died soon after Reg paid me a visit. He seemed pretty distraught. He came into the kitchen and sat down. I made him a cup of tea, and soon he was telling me what his mother had told him just before she died. It turned out that his father was not his real father. Reg's mother had worked as a land army girl, just after the 2nd world war, on a farm in Witney. Apparently there were about 4 girls working there. The farmer's wife had, what we know today as Alzheimer's disease, but back then little was known about the condition. Anyway the farmer started an affair with Reg's mother when she was just 18, and she became pregnant. Now in those days this was frowned upon. So she was moved to a dingy flat in London, where she gave birth to Reg, all paid for by the farmer When she was well enough she moved back to Brightwell and lived with her sister. Soon afterwards the farmer died in a car crash, so all contact with him was lost. When Reg was 5 years old his mother met a local farm labourer and he proposed. But he wanted young Reg put into a home. His mother would only agree to marry the labourer if he adopted Reg as his own, which he did reluctantly.

"So" Reg said, "that is why my stepfather did not take any interest in me and why he was always beating me, he felt he had been blackmailed into marriage because of me." After Reg had unbottled all his feelings, he seemed to calm down.

"All these years and she never told me," he said. "I feel totally let down." We talked for a couple of hours until Reg decided to leave.

"Let's keep in touch" he said as he climbed into his car. He waved goodbye and sped off down the road. It was a month later that I heard he sold his house at a loss and moved back into Brightwell. He bought a cottage in Slade End, right next to the house he had been brought up as a child. I suppose the next time I saw him was about six months later when he phoned and asked if I could meet him in the Red Lion public house at Brightwell. When I got there I looked around, and at first could not see him. And then an old man in a raincoat put his hand on my shoulder.

"Hello Brian" he said. I spun around and there was Reg, he looked a bit bedraggled with a good week's growth on his face. "Let's sit over here" he said pulling me into the snug, "where it's quiet." We sat down and a young waitress came over.

"Can I get you anything to eat?" she asked.

"No thanks" said Reg, "just 2 pints of lager." She came back a few minutes later and put the lagers down on the table. "Is there anything else I can get you"? she said.

"No thanks," said Reg as he sipped his lager. After the waitress had left and Reg had drunk half of his pint, he made sure nobody was within earshot and then began to tell me about his amazing experience.

PART 2

Reg liked walking and if he'd had an argument with his wife he would either go to the pub or go for a long walk to cool off. On this particular morning it was sunny but misty, although this was not uncommon as Didcot Power Station was only about 1 mile away. The giant cooling towers sent hot gases and steam up into the atmosphere causing all sorts of peculiar weather conditions. As he left the house he went past the farm up the hill past the Free Church and into Bakers Lane. He called in to St James Church to see his parent's grave. He then carried on following the road on to a lane that went up to the top road. He crossed the newly built bypass and then took the old bridle path that went up to Green Hill. This path was quite overgrown, but was still accessible. About a hundred yards in, the path went into a small gully with high banks on either side. It was always muddy here and the mist hung low in the gully. As he made his way along he noticed a strange orange light coming from the old apple store high up on the bank.

This orchard was once owned by Mr Sheard, but the orchard and store had been neglected for years and was now almost impenetrable. Reg pulled himself up the bank, and climbed through a gap in the fence. Then he forced his way through the undergrowth to the side door of the apple store. The strange orange glow was coming from inside the store. He turned the door knob and pushed the door, it didn't budge. After all these years he thought it must be rusted up so turned the door knob again and gave a hearty shove with his shoulder. The door swung open. At first the orange glow hurt his eyes. He shielded them with his hands until he had grown accustomed to the light.

There were no windows in the store, just one room about 14 feet by 10 feet with a pitched, tiled roof. Empty apple boxes littered the floor, and on the back wall was another door, from where the orange glow was seeping, lighting the whole room. Reg stood there for a few minutes not knowing what to do. He hadn't passed another door on the outside. He walked slowly backwards until he bumped into the open entrance door that he had just passed through. He stepped outside and made his way back around the other end of the store. There was no door to be seen, only ivy and brambles growing up the walls. He made his way back inside the apple store. The door was still there as was the strange orange glow. Reg felt himself being drawn towards it, his hand turned the door knob and the door suddenly opened outwards.

The orange light had disappeared and he was looking into a beautiful orchard. He glanced back into the darkened room but could not see any other door. Reg stepped out into the orchard. Something was different, not just the orchard, he felt different: younger, fitter and happier. He walked through the orchard admiring the apple blossom and the neatly cut trees. He felt the long sweet-smelling grass brushing his shins. He looked down at his feet, but instead of a pair of old faded jeans, two small legs protruded from a pair of short trousers with grey ankle socks and brown sandals. Reg reached down and touched his legs then pinched himself. It hurt, so he knew he wasn't dreaming. He examined his other clothing. He was dressed in a white sleeveless shirt under a thin grey jumper. He felt his face and hair. His face felt smaller with a good crop of blond curly hair hanging down to his shoulders.

Reg didn't have a mirror, but it suddenly dawned on him that he had changed into a small child. He didn't feel any different in his mind, he wasn't going mad, but it did feel strange as he walked through the grass. It was when he came to the gate at the bottom of the orchard that he knew something was seriously wrong. He tried to open the gate but his hand passed right through it and he was able to walk through the gate without opening it. He stood by the side of the road wondering what was happening. Where was the new bypass? He looked across the old high road at the top of Bell Lane and watched the old pub, busy with customers. He knew the Bell Public House had closed many years ago and had been turned into a private dwelling. So if this was real, then he must be back in the mid-1950s. Reg crossed the road and glanced in through the windows at the men enjoying their midday pint. He quickened his pace and followed the route back to his house. As he was walking it felt strange, as if he were walking on air. When he stamped his foot down on the road it did not make a sound.

He pinched himself hard again and it hurt. I can't be dreaming this, he thought to himself, but he was a little afraid as he carried on down Bakers Lane. As he passed St James Church he passed through the gate and went in to see his parents' grave. It wasn't there; the patch where his parents had been buried just over a year ago was a neatly mown patch of grass. He sat down, his head in a whirl. Then he noticed a man walking towards him. As he got nearer he could see it was the vicar walking down the path. Reg didn't recognise him, but he jumped to his feet and went towards him holding out his arm to shake hands. But as he got nearer he realised something was odd: the vicar had no depth and looked like a hologram. Reg stopped with his hand held out, but the vicar passed right through him and carried on walking.

Reg shuddered turned around and shouted "Excuse me!" but there was no response. He felt a cold sweat sweeping through his body, had he died and come back as a ghost? He pulled himself together and decided to go home. As he got back on the road an old orange bus with the words Chilton Queens written along the side swept around the corner. Reg stood mesmerized; he knew the bus firm had not operated since the seventies, over forty years ago. He stood in the road looking at the disappearing bus. As he turned a car drove straight through him. It didn't brake or swerve, it felt strange like a cold chill penetrating his body He could see the driver, a cigarette dangling from his mouth, as the car sped off. Was he a ghost? Why hadn't the driver seen him? He carried on past the Free Church and down the hill into Slade End. He got to the farm just as a tractor pulled out. He stopped dead, eyes bulging. He couldn't believe it. His father was driving the tractor. Reg waved he was only four feet away, but his father drove straight past. Reg stood in disbelief looking at his father disappearing into the distance. He continued on to his cottage and walked up the path to his front gate. A small boy of about six was playing on his trike, loading twigs on to the little trailer he was towing. Reg knelt down.

"Hello young man, what's your name?" As the young boy turned Reg recognized him immediately; he was wearing a grey jumper over a white shirt, a small pair of legs stuck out of a pair of grey shorts. It was his younger self.

Reg fell back in disbelief and lay on the grass watching himself playing with his trike. His early memories all came flooding back. He remembered the little trike and trailer that was given to him on his sixth birthday, it was second-hand but he didn't mind, to him it was a lorry towing a trailer full of logs like his uncle's in the timber yard at the other end of the village. Reg reached out to touch the young boy, but he touched thin air it was all a hologram nothing was real. But he felt real, the grass he was sitting on felt wet and as he stood up he had a damp patch on the backside of his shorts. Reg suddenly remembered his mother: if his father was alive then his mother must be. He crossed the road to the house where he had grown up all those years ago. All of a sudden he was standing in the kitchen watching his mother preparing the evening meal. She didn't look any different. Bruce the black Labrador was asleep in his basket. "Hello Mum," he heard himself say, but he did not get any response. He stayed in the kitchen for quite some time watching his mother until the door suddenly opened and in strode a rather portly man, his shirt undone to the waist.

"Where's that little bastard? He should be in by now," his father said.

"He's playing on his trike in the path next to the fields" said his mother, "he'll be in shortly."

"I'll go and get him" said his father. He strode down the garden and onto the little path adjoining the fields. Reg knew what was about to happen, he followed his father until he reached the little boy playing with his trike.

"I was just coming home, Dad" the boy said. "I have filled my trailer with some sticks so Mum can light the fire." His father took off his belt and kicked, out knocking over the trike and little trailer filled with sticks.

"You'll come now you little bastard" he swung the belt round and caught the little boy across the back. Reg's eyes swelled up with tears, he knew how much that belt hurt. He tried to punch his father but he just punched thin air. He watched helplessly as the little boy ran back to the house crying. He followed his father back to the house. When he arrived the little boy was sitting at the kitchen table. His tearstained face froze as his father stepped into the kitchen.

"Have you been beating that boy again?" asked his mother.

"I only gave him a clip" said his father "he's just a little cry-baby."

"You are too hard on the boy" said his mother. "He's only 6 years old." Reg realized he could not make contact with his mother and tell her the truth about his father. She could not see or hear him He could not bear to relive the suffering, so he left. He made his way back up to the old apple store. The orange light was still visible under the door; he pulled the door open and stepped inside. He was now back in the old store shed. The old apple boxes were still strewn across the floor, but the orange light had disappeared. He was a man again, dressed in the same clothes as before He opened the only door that was now visible and stepped out into the old neglected apple orchard. It was dusk and he realized he had been gone for about eight hours.

Reg paused; took a last swig of lager and said "Well, do you think it was all a dream, Brian?"

I sat thinking for a while and said "If you think it was real, then it was real." We sat in the pub and had another lager before I left, that was the last time I saw Reg for another year

PART 3

Reg had rung me a few times, but we did not meet up for a drink until a year later. I bought him a pint as he looked as if he couldn't afford it. He was very scruffy and unshaven.

"Good God man, what has happened to you?" I asked him as we sat down. He swigged the beer down as if there was no tomorrow.

"If you buy me a double whisky, then I'll tell you" he said. Now I know Reg never touched whisky—he hated the stuff, but I bought him a double as he had asked. He took a mouthful, swilled it around his mouth as though it was pure nectar, before swallowing it. He sat for a few minutes, and then suddenly said "I've left my wife."

"For God's sake, why?" was the only thing I could think of saying.

"Because I caught her in bed with a younger man" he said.

I could see he was having trouble keeping his emotions under control, but he told me the whole story with tears in his eyes. Apparently the marriage had been breaking down over the last year but he had ignored the signs. First their sex life diminished and then fizzled out altogether; her excuse was they were too old for that sort of thing. Then kissing was not on the agenda, a peck on the cheek was all that was permitted and very soon they were not talking to each other. So Reg would often leave for work, very unhappy. Then one day he thought he would cheer his wife up and take her out to dinner. He rushed home stopping off at the petrol station to buy a large bouquet of flowers. He thought he would surprise her so he left his van on the road, crept up the footpath and tried opening the front door, but it was locked. He thought that was strange, as his wife's car was still in the carport.

He crept around the back and tried the patio doors. They slid quietly open, he slipped inside and listened. Faint noises were coming from upstairs Reg tiptoed upstairs the noises were coming from behind the main bedroom door. He listened for a while, he then recognized the heavy sighing noises his wife made while making love. He could feel the anger building up until he could stand it no more He opened the door and bust into the room His wife was on her back and a young man was straddling her naked body. He stood staring for a few moments trying to understand why his wife, his partner for 40years had betrayed him like this. But instead of punching the man or hitting him Reg could feel tears running down the side of his face, he didn't say anything but left the room so they wouldn't see him crying. He got back in his van and drove around for a while, his mind in utter confusion and that's when he rang me.

He took the last remaining mouthful of whisky and said "She wants a divorce on the grounds of mental cruelty, can you believe that? She's having an affair and she's blaming me."

"Looks like you could do with another drink" I said, which he gladly accepted. "Reg, I don't know what to say" I continued, "you will have to pull yourself together and sort this mess out, or else she will take you for everything you own" He drank the whisky down in one mouthful.

"I must go" he said, looking at his watch, and got up to leave.

"If there is anything I can do, just call me" I said as he waved goodbye and got in his van and drove off.

It was two months later that I heard that he had been declared bankrupt. I tried to call his mobile, but was informed that the number was no longer available. I drove over to Brightwell to see him. A large Under Offer sign was fixed to the side of the house. I walked up the garden path and knocked on the front door, there was no answer. I peered in through the lounge window and could see all the furniture had been removed. So I rang the estate agents who were selling the property and asked them if they knew the whereabouts of Reginald White. After I had explained who I was and how worried I had become about his mental state, the receptionist informed me that Mrs White had instructed them to sell the property as she had divorced her husband and he had moved away from the area. It was then I reported his disappearance to the police. They took a description of Reg, and they said they would keep an eye out for him and ring me if they had any information.

PART 4

One cold night in November my wife and I had just gone to bed when I heard a loud knocking on the front door. My wife was already asleep, so I put on my dressing gown, went downstairs and opened the front door. An old man with a big bushy beard and large dirty raincoat stood in the doorway, an old woolly hat pulled down over his ears. I noticed he was holding a half empty whisky bottle in his hand and he smelt awful.

"What do you want?" I asked angrily, "we were both asleep and you've woken us up!"

"I am sorry Brian, but you are my only friend," he replied.

I immediately knew it was Reg. I could see he needed help, so invited him in. After he had had a shower, shaved off his beard and got dressed in some clothes I gave him, he looked like his normal self, apart from his weight loss. I cooked him some sausage, egg and chips, which he tucked into greedily and, after a large cup of tea he seemed to relax.

"You had better tell me what's happened to you and where you have been" I said. "I have already reported you missing to the local police."

"I know I should have told you, Brian" Reg replied, "but I have been back twice since I last saw you."

At first I didn't know what he was rambling on about and then it dawned on me, he was talking about his dream. We went into the lounge and, after another cup of tea Reg recounted what had happen to him since we last met up.

"The last time I crossed over into the other world, things had changed" said Reg. "That's where I have been for the last month."

"Changed? What do you mean?" I asked, getting closer to Reg so I could hear everything clearly.

"Well, I walk past the apple store quite regularly, but there has been no orange light until recently. So when it appeared I crossed over into the parallel world."

"That's what it is" said Reg. "A parallel world only in the past, it's not a dream, every time I go back time is catching up. The first time was when I was six, the second time was when I was sixteen and the last time I was twenty-six. But each time I go back it gets more real. Objects were solid, not holograms, people spoke to me and it hurt when I walked into things."

"Didn't anybody recognize you?" I interrupted.

"Not really," said Reg. "I disguised myself a bit and didn't reply to anybody I recognized, they must have thought I was very rude."

"But where have you been living" I asked.

"I befriended an old lady" Reg continued, "she sat next to me on a park bench and we got chatting, her husband had recently died and she was very lonely in her big old house.

And when I told her I was a builder and looking for somewhere to stay, she offered me a room in exchange for some renovation work, so it worked out pretty well. I was able to watch my wife and family growing up from a distance. I thought about introducing myself as a long lost cousin but I didn't think that would work. So I decided to come back to the real world, just to say goodbye really"

"Goodbye? What do you mean, Reg?" I blurted out.

"I have got it all worked out" said Reg. "Next time I have the opportunity to cross over into the other world, I am going back for good." He paused, "Next time I go back I will be thirty-six if my calculations are correct. I should be in my prime, when I was the most successful. My parents will have passed away and I can introduce myself as a long lost brother to Reg. He will probably believe me, as mother lied to him before about his father. Anyway I can think up a story about being adopted at birth to explain why I have suddenly appeared on the scene, so to speak."

"And when I have gained his confidence I can steer him in the right direction and avoid his bankruptcy and marriage breakdown." He paused again and took a deep breath. "Don't you see Brian? I have the opportunity to change the future." He stopped and stared into my eyes looking for approval. I was trying to take it all in and was unprepared when he stopped talking.

"Well, what do you think?" he said when I didn't answer him.

I gathered my thoughts, I wanted to believe him, but the story he had told me was just too incredible

"Reg, are you taking any drugs or medication for your depression that might explain these fantasies?" His face suddenly contorted in anger.

"You don't believe a word I have said, do you?" he shouted. "You're the only true friend I can talk to and you think it's all in my imagination." He picked his coat up and stormed out of the house. I shouted after him, but he didn't look back. I thought of going after him, but a movement from inside the house stopped me.

"What's all the noise about?" enquired my bleary-eyed wife who had just woken up. I looked at my watch and realized we had been talking all night; it was 6.15 am and dawn was just breaking.

"It's all right, dear" I replied, "it was Reg, he has just left. He had nowhere to go, so I let him stay the night"

I searched all day for Reg, driving around the local pubs and doss houses. I feared my disbelief may have pushed him over the edge and I was worried that he might harm himself. I never saw or heard from him again. The police were still looking for him one month later and put him on their missing list. I didn't know what to believe.

Then one afternoon I was taking the dog for a walk up Green Hill. The weather was changing for the worse. Dark storm clouds were gathering overhead and a thick mist covered the ground. I hurried on, wanting to get back home before the weather broke. I took a short cut down the hill and suddenly found myself walking through a deep gully. I could just make out a faint orange glow high up on the bank. My dog ran up the bank and disappeared, so I had to clamber up after it. When I reached the top, there was the old apple store with a distinct orange glow radiating from inside, just as Reg had described. As I walked around the building the dog was pawing at the door, so I put his lead on and looked at the door. Should I take a peek inside, just to prove Reg had a vivid imagination? I felt my hand grab the door handle and turn it. The door swung open freely and the orange light blinded me for a second.

When my eyes had grown accustomed to the light, I could see the dog was sniffing an old shabby raincoat. I picked it up and knew straight away it was Reg's. I looked at the other door where the orange light was penetrating around the door frame. I reached out, intending to have a little peek behind the door. It wouldn't do any harm. I didn't have to go through it, just see what was on the other side. There was a sudden pull on the lead; my dog seemed to know what I wanted to do. Was I in some sort of trance? I felt very lightheaded, but then the dog started barking which instantly brought me back to reality. I turned and went outside into the overcast evening; it was just starting to rain. I slipped Reg's raincoat over my head, clambered down the bank and made my way home.

I took the raincoat into the police station the next morning. After a DNA test a week later it was confirmed that it belonged to Reginald White, missing for over five weeks. The police examined the apple store and the door handle was dusted for fingerprints, but there was no evidence that Reg had ever been there.

Was Reg telling the truth? Had he passed over into a parallel world and found he could change his past? I have my doubts, but a week later I was out walking the dog and decided to take the short cut up Green Hill. It was a nice sunny afternoon but as soon as I entered the gully and got closer to the apple store it became quite cold and misty. It was then I noticed a man coming towards me. He was wearing a shabby old raincoat and hat. As he got nearer my heart began to beat faster, had Reg returned to visit me? As the man passed me I could see it wasn't him.

I said "Good morning!" but the tramp just made a grunting noise and carried on walking. Then I had a premonition. I turned around and saw the tramp clambering up the bank to the apple store. I was too far away to see if there was any orange glow. Had Reg confided in an old acquaintance and told him his secret? Or was the tramp just looking for a nice cosy shelter for the night? The answer to that question, I'm afraid, we will never know.

THE ANAEROBIC DIGESTER

CHAPTER 1

John Winchester and his wife Gillian had lived in Potash Lane for almost fourteen years. He had retired from the building trade to concentrate on writing books, and found it was the ideal location for him to drift away in his own imagination. There were about ten houses in the Lane, starting with a large old house that once belonged to the RAF in the 2nd World War. The house had been converted into a Charitable Trust that looked after terminally ill and mentally damaged adults. The quiet lane was ideal for the patients to cycle up and down on their special trikes, accompanied by their carers. Next to them was the local team's football field, which was used most weekends. John and his wife lived next door, separated by a small field. Next to his property were two pretty semidetached cottages, set back from the road. Clare and Dennis Jefferies lived in the first house and June Collins in the next; beyond that lay a newly modernized house, owned by the local builder. Across the road a modern bungalow nestled among the apple trees. Further down the road was a detached house surrounded by a large lawn and at the far end of the lane was a large manor house owned by the local farmer and landowner.

One late December morning a letter from the local County Council was pushed through the letterbox. John picked it up and opened it. He didn't understand all the technical jargon and threw the letter on his desk, intending to read it later. That evening his neighbour, Dennis, knocked on his front door.

"Have you read this letter?" he said as John opened the door. Dennis was holding an opened letter in his hand, but before John had time to answer his question he continued "They are going to build an anaerobic digester in the cherry orchard, right next to our houses."

John looked at his concerned face, and asked "What's an anaerobic digester?"

"I can't explain it to you now" he said. "I must go and organize a meeting before it's too late."

"Too late for what?" John shouted after him, but he had disappeared into his house.

The next day Carole Shelby and her husband, who lived in a large house that lay back from the main road, organized a meeting at her house. Quite a few of the neighbours attended the meeting. Carole laid an aerial photograph of the proposed development on the table.

"This is what the council want to erect right here in the cherry orchard," said Carole. "And we have to reply to their letter by 14th January if we want to object to the development."

"That only gives us three weeks" said Dennis. "I bet the planners tried to sneak this through over Christmas so nobody would notice it."

They all studied the photograph and the proposed development. Six large circular containers, each six metres high, were to be erected right next to the lane making easy access for the large articulated lorries bringing food and chicken waste from London. The waste material was then stored in open concrete pens until it had rotted, then it was loaded into the containers to ferment and turned into methane gas. This was then pumped into large underground storage tanks. Eventually the gas would be pumped into the national grid system.

"Well, what can we do about this?" said Clare. "We cannot allow this to happen. The smell and noise from the lorries will be tremendous!"

"I could look into the past history of Potash lane and see if there is anything we could use to dissuade the council from giving their approval," said Dennis.

"I'll arrange a meeting with the parish council" said Carole, "and we must organise a protest committee." They all agreed and after a cup of tea made their way home. Carole kept her word and set up a meeting the following week with the parish council, after delivering flyers about the event to all the neighbouring houses. The meeting went very well, a lot of local people attended, and most of the parish councillors gave their support to the protestors. Carole made a rallying speech, and they all left the meeting feeling rather proud of themselves.

The next morning Dennis was sitting at his desk browsing through the past history of the surrounding area. Suddenly he called Clare into the office.

"Look at this Clare," he said. "Apparently this place was once a Roman settlement called Milltown Hill. It's thought that a large windmill was used to grind the local farmers' corn and wheat crops and the flour was sold in the town. There were some archaeological digs about fifty years ago and they found coins, pots and milling tools, and they are all displayed at the Ashmolean Museum in Oxford." Dennis read a few more pages, and then gasped. "And that's not all, they also found whole skeletons in a burial site," then he paused, "but it doesn't say exactly where they were found."

"Couldn't we present this to the Council and say this is an archaeological site and needs to be preserved?" asked Clare. Dennis agreed and rang Carole with the news.

"Surely the County Council would have to listen to us now with this evidence" said Carole "Then they'll withdraw the planning application, all we have to do is wait and see if we have done enough."

Two weeks went by before another letter arrived from the Council, saying they were reviewing the planning application.

"Reviewing the planning application?" said Carole. "Haven't the Council taken our protest seriously? I'll arrange a meeting with our local MP, maybe we can get him on our side."

"And I'll arrange a photo-shoot with the local paper," said Clare. "A bit of publicity might help." They all decided to meet the following week and discuss the progress after the photoshoot.

Six days later Carole emailed everyone to arrange a meeting at her place at 7pm that evening. After everyone had arrived and made themselves comfortable around the large dining room table, Carole stood up. She was very upset.

"I have been talking directly to the County Council over the last two days" she said "and have finally forced their hand to give us the verdict on the planning application. I received this letter in the evening post." She held up the letter. "It seems" she continued, "that after all our efforts the Council have rejected our appeal, and the Anaerobic Digester will now go ahead." There was silence for a few seconds before the news finally sank in.

"Do we know when the project will start?" asked Dennis. Carole read through the letter quickly.

"It doesn't give an actual start date" replied Carole. "It just says work will begin mid-February."

"That's only four weeks away!" said Maria "What can we do in that short time?"

"We can always sit down in front of the lorries," said Dennis. "Then they'll know we mean business!" They all left Carole's house feeling totally dejected, and agreed to work on a plan to stop this industrial development from starting. The decision was made the following week. John had noticed a red band had been painted around two of the old chestnut trees lining the lane. He rang Carole and the others for another meeting.

"I think the trees have been marked for felling" said John, "to allow the artic lorries easier access into the site." He looked around at the others' expressionless faces. "Don't you see?" continued John "This has given us a great opportunity." The others still didn't understand what he was talking about. So he continued "We could camp out in the trees, they wouldn't be able to cut them down then."

"A bit like Swampy," said Clare. They all looked at her for an explanation. "You know, the man that led the Newbury Bypass protesters about ten years ago He camped up in the trees to stop them being felled. Well, we could do the same." As he was a retired carpenter, John agreed to build a platform with some sort of shelter overhead.

"I could build it high up in the branches" said John, "with a rope ladder so we could pull it up behind us." Everybody thought this a great idea.

"After all" said John, "if they can't cut the trees down, they can't get into the site."

Everybody left the meeting feeling a bit hopeful that this action would get some TV coverage and the planners would have to consider a new site location.

Over the next couple of days John, with the help of Dennis, built the small platform high up in the largest tree. It was large enough for one person to lie down in a sleeping bag without rolling off the platform. The roof was just two sheets of plywood lashed together with rope, it was watertight to an extent but in a high wind it wasn't an ideal place to be. But it was finished and John decided to try it out first, and the others agreed to each do a six hour shift. It was a bit uncomfortable at first, but after a while John found just the right spot and fell asleep. It was six in the morning when Clare shouted up at John and woke him up. John threw the rope ladder down and they swapped places. It was Carole's shift next. Then Dennis did the 6pm to midnight slot. They thought that was the fairest way so the girls did not have to spend a cold and sometimes wet night up in the tree.

It was 20th of February when the tree surgeons arrived to fell the trees at 8 o' clock in the morning. Clare was up the tree watching the men getting their chainsaws ready. They started cutting the lower branches to scare her.

"Come on down, lady!" said Andy the foreman. "You've made your protest, now let us do our job."

"You're not cutting this tree down!" shouted Clare "I've phoned the others and they'll be here any minute." Dennis and John came running down the road a few minutes later.

"I've phoned the Oxford Mail" shouted Dennis "and they're sending out a photographer, so don't you dare cut that tree down!" After a lot of shouting the police arrived fifteen minutes later, and tried to calm the situation.

"Look here," said Andy handing the constable a piece of paper. "That's our authority to cut this tree down." After reading the document the constable shouted up to Clare.

"Look Clare, why don't you come on down and we can talk this through peacefully?"

"I am not coming down until you have all gone," she screamed.

"Well, what are you going to do, Constable?" said Andy. "We're supposed to have this tree down and removed before the contractors arrive tomorrow morning."

The Constable rang his Sergeant for some advice and six minutes later a fire engine arrived, just as the photographer pulled up in his car. The fire engine driver raised the ladder to within two feet of the platform, and a fireman climbed the ladder. He jumped onto the platform and tried to grab Clare.

"Stay away from me or I will jump!" she shouted. The fireman retreated two steps and Clare seemed to be in command of the situation. But as soon as she stepped away from the edge he grabbed her and lifted her over his shoulder. He brought her down the ladder, screaming and kicking. The photographer wasted no time in capturing the whole incident on film. The police held Dennis and the others back while the tree was felled. Clare was in tears.

"All this was for nothing!" she cried. The others tried to comfort her, but could only look on as the tree was cut up and taken away in a lorry. The next morning Clare was on the front page of the Oxford Mail. It wasn't a very flattering picture, with her being brought down the ladder bottom first, with the headlines: What a BUM protest from the residents of Potash Lane.

"Why can't the papers support us more?" wailed Clare "Instead of making a joke of it all?" Dennis tried to console her, but just made the situation worse.

"We've lost the battle, haven't we?" she cried. Dennis put his arms around her and whispered "We're down, but we're not out yet."

The residents of Potash Lane tried to block the road to stop the lorries and excavators from getting on site, but the police thwarted their plans by placing barricades across the lane preventing anybody from interfering with the contractors.

PART 2

THE CONSTRUCTION

Keith McKellen was in charge of the construction team. This was mainly made up of Irish immigrants who had no family and other men who had been in trouble and wanted to keep a low profile. Keith liked this situation, as it meant they would do exactly as they were told and work long hours without complaining. He had worked with this team before, travelling around Britain building the digesters. Most of the men lived in caravans on site. Mick Feeney and James Patterson were both excavator drivers. Brian Kelly and his younger brother Daniel were steel fabricators and Shawn Murphy was the labourer, but he could turn his hand to almost anything from driving dumpers, to bolting the structures together. Keith McKellen was a hard man but he knew he had a good bunch of men in his team. At the last site they had worked on they had completed the construction in four months. After the men had set up their caravans, Keith called them into the site office.

"Look lads, I know you worked damned hard on that last job," he said, "But I want to finish this project in three months, and I will give you all a big bonus if you can do it." The men were thrilled with the news, but knew Keith would be pushing them even harder. The next morning they started levelling the site. They had hired two local lorry drivers to shift the soil to a landfill site at Chilton only five miles away.

As soon as Mick dug the first bucket deep into the earth he felt a strange feeling, as though he shouldn't be doing this and it was wrong, but he continued and between them they had levelled the site by midday. After a quick lunch down at Murphy's café in Steventon, they returned on site to start digging the giant hole for the underground storage tanks. But the deeper Mick dug the more uneasy he became. He stopped the excavator and looked around him. Across the road he could see the large old house converted into a home for the mental and autistic patients. Up in the top far right window he noticed a face watching him, but he didn't take much notice. He started the excavator and carried on digging. By evening the hole had been half dug. Mick kept glancing at the top window across the road, the face was still there peering over the window sill.

That night Mick had a nightmare. He dreamt dead people were coming out of the ground all around him, and pushing his caravan into the hole. He awoke and sat bolt upright, his body covered in sweat, he felt the caravan moving, swaying to and fro. He got up and rushed outside, it was dark but the moon illuminated the tall chestnut trees standing on each side of the lane. There was quite a cold breeze blowing across the site moving his caravan back and forth. Nobody was around, all the other men were sound asleep in their caravans, and he could just hear their snoring above the breeze. He felt a little better knowing his mates were only feet away. As he was about to get back in his caravan he looked across at the old house across the road. A light was on in the top right hand window and a face was still there staring at him. Mick quickly closed the door and went to bed. He didn't mention his nightmare to the men the next morning, after all he was a grown man, and grown men weren't supposed to have nightmares so he kept it to himself. After a cup of tea and some toast the men started back to work. Mick glanced up at the window across the road but he couldn't see any face, which made him feel at ease.

"Come on lads," said Keith. "I want this hole finished today so we can get the steelwork started." Mick climbed into his excavator and started digging, but he hadn't dug down very far before he stopped.

"Here Guv, you had better come and see this!" he shouted across to Keith who was helping Brian get the steel reinforcing ready. Both men ran over.

"Look down there," said Mick pointing to a bone sticking out of the soil. They both climbed down the ladder into the three metre deep hole.

"Do you think it's a human bone?" said Mick feeling a bit uneasy. Keith examined the bone, and then kicked at the surrounding soil, another bone was exposed, and then in the corner he unearthed a skeleton.

"Oh my God!" shouted Mick. "We've only dug up a burial site!"

"Keep your voice down!" said Keith. "We don't want the authorities to hear about this. The whole site will have to be closed and examined. That could take months and we would lose that big fat bonus we were promised. You're nearly down to the correct depth then we can put the steel reinforcing in and concrete over before anybody sees it, OK?"

Mick reluctantly agreed and climbed out of the hole. He looked up at the window across the road. The face was back there again, had it seen what they had uncovered? He quickly climbed into the excavator and started digging. He thought he might go over to the house when he had finished and ask who it was that was watching him. At midday they all decided to go to Murphy's café again.

"Come on, let's walk there" said Keith. "It's not far."

"I'm going to stay and finish this," said Mick. "I'll have it finished by the time you get back."

The other men hurried off down the road for a nice mug of tea and a fried lunch, leaving Mick alone digging out the final bucketfuls of soil. There were a lot of bones and skulls scattered around the bottom of the hole. Mick had to be right on the edge of the hole to be able to reach the last bucketful. Suddenly the excavator began to move forward as if it were being pulled by an unknown force He just had enough time to open the arm before the excavator was pulled over the edge and into the hole. The front bucket dug into the earth flinging Mick through the opened front screen onto the ground. He lay still for a few seconds wondering what had happened. He turned over and lay on his back and saw the five ton excavator was balanced precariously on the front bucket and the tracks which had dug into the bank, and he was directly underneath the machine. He tried to get up, but something was holding him. He looked down at his ankles; bony skeleton-like hands were grasping him firmly, pulling him into the soil. He screamed and kicked out, but more hands were grabbing him, pulling him under.

He cried out, "Help, help me somebody!" But his mates were all down at the café enjoying their well-earned meal, oblivious to their friend's cry for help. Mick glanced out of the hole and just caught the sight of the face smiling at him through the window, before he was dragged kicking and screaming underground. It was 12.45 before the men returned and immediately saw the excavator sticking out of the hole wedged onto its front bucket,

"Quick, go and see if Mick's alright!" shouted Keith. But after searching the area there was no sign of him.

"Perhaps somebody's taken him to hospital" said Brian.

"Let's get this excavator out of the hole before anybody sees it," said Keith. "Then we can search for Mick." They quickly tied straps around the excavator and pulled it clear of the hole with the other excavator. Keith rang around the local hospitals and health clinics. He even went back to the café and asked the waitresses if they had seen Mick, but nobody had so he returned to the site. Brian and Danny had covered the remaining bones that were visible with soil. Danny had an uncanny feeling that the bottom of the hole was getting softer under foot and his boots seemed to pull him into the ground. He clambered out of the hole and passed Brian the large reinforcing sheets. When they were spread over the bottom of the hole, the sensation disappeared. By the end of the day all the steel fabrication had been finished and they were ready to pour the concrete.

"I've ordered two loads for tomorrow morning," said Keith, "and then we can cover all this mess up and no one will be any the wiser."

They all went to bed that night wondering what had happened to Mick. It was about midnight when Brian was woken by somebody calling his name. He couldn't hear very clearly but it was definitely coming from outside. He quickly got dressed and went outside. It was pitch black, there was no moon only the breeze whistling through the old chestnut trees. The voice could be heard clearer now.

"Brian, help me!" It sounded like Mick's voice.

"Mick, is that you?" he shouted. He wished he had a torch, but the voice was coming from the hole so he stepped nearer and looked over the edge, beneath the reinforcing he could see movement. It was too dark for him to see clearly, but the reinforcing bars were being pushed upwards. All of a sudden something grabbed his ankles and he was pulled head first onto the steel bars at the bottom of the hole, he was knocked out and lay still. The next morning Danny found the body and raised the alarm. Brian had fallen heavily on a reinforcing bar sticking up at the side of the structure. The bar had penetrated his neck and he had bled to death.

"We must call an ambulance," said Danny. "They might be able to save him!"

Keith put his arm around Danny's shoulder. "There's nothing we can do for him Danny, he's dead," said Keith. "Feel his body, it's stone cold." They lifted Brian's body out of the hole and placed him in the site office.

"We'll leave the body here until after the concrete has been poured," said Keith. "Then we'll phone for an ambulance." He looked at the men's shocked faces. "It's for the best" he continued. "If anybody catches us concreting over this site then we will be in a lot of trouble." He looked at his watch. "The lorries will be here in a minute, let's get the job done and we can all relax." They all agreed with Keith, although Danny thought he was a bit unsympathetic toward his brother.

By ten o clock both lorries had emptied the concrete into the base of the hole and the men had levelled it off. When the ambulance arrived there was no trace of any burial ground. The paramedics thought it a bit odd that the body was not reported sooner. But after Keith's explanation they seemed satisfied and left with the body. Danny was distraught about his brother's death.

"There's something evil here" cried Danny "I can feel it all around us." Keith decided to take them all to the nearest pub, at least if they were drunk the pain would be easier. But as they were sipping their pints, Keith wondered what dreadful thing had happened to Mick. Why had he not contacted him? Had he just walked out without getting paid? It was three in the afternoon when the four men arrived back on site. Danny was very drunk and could hardly walk.

"Let's sleep it off until the morning" said Keith, "and then we can have an early start." Danny didn't hear what Keith had said as he was already in a deep sleep. The next morning Danny had accepted his brother's death. Now they were down to four men they would have to work flat out to finish on time, but things didn't go to plan. Tools seemed to be moved into different places. Keys went missing and, most worrying of all, there seemed to be uneasy feeling when Keith and the others built the retaining wall around the hole. Nobody saw anything suspicious, but the hole did claim another life before it was finished. The two excavators were lowering the massive gas storage tank onto the concrete base. Danny was on the side holding on to the guide ropes trying to drop the tank into position on the retaining bolts. One of the chains holding the tank suddenly snapped, Danny was pulled into the hole and the tank slid out of the other chain and crushed him. Keith had to close the site down until the safety officers had investigated the accident. He was beginning to think these deaths were no accident. He had already lost two men and one was still missing.

A week later Keith was allowed to reopen the site and had to hire four local men to help finish the job. Even by cutting a few corners and missing some of the hidden work, the job was completed two weeks behind schedule. So none of the men received the big bonus they were expecting. But Keith was glad the job was finished and he was able to hand over the site to the operating firm, PNG Energy. The anaerobic digester was officially opened a week later by the County Council, much to the disgust of the local residents.

PART 3

THE CONCLUSION

Toby Maguire lived in the Trust Centre across the road from the anaerobic digester. He was a thirty year man who had been involved in a dreadful car accident that had left him brain damaged and slightly handicapped. Toby had lived in the house for three years and was being looked after by his carer, Rosie Williams. Even though he had the mind of a ten year old and was slightly paralyzed in his left arm, he could still ride his three wheeled trike down the road, followed closely by Rosie. Toby had his own room on the top floor, with a big window overlooking the anaerobic digester site.

He had watched the men build the site from his window and had seen the terrible accidents, but was too afraid to say anything so had kept quiet about his little secret. It was a glorious Sunday morning and there were not many deliveries of waste material to the plant that day. As Toby had not been out on his trike for over a month, Rosie decided he needed cheering up, so she got the new white trike out ready as a surprise.

"Shall we go for a bike ride today, Toby?" asked Rosie. "The roads are not too muddy and I can walk behind you." Toby was very excited and climbed onto the trike. He started pedalling the trike up the road, with Rosie following close behind. He had ridden about 100 yards when he suddenly stopped opposite the entrance to the waste site.

"We can't go any further," said Toby.

"Why not?" replied Rosie, who had nearly walked into the back of the trike.

"Because of the bony people" said Toby. "They won't like it"

"What bony people?" asked Rosie.

"The bony people that live over there," said Toby, pointing over to the waste digester site. Rosie stared over to where Toby was pointing, but couldn't see anything, so she started walking ahead.

"Come on slowcoach, we'll walk to the end of the road and back again," said Rosie.

Then Toby started crying. "Don't go Miss, or else the bony people will pull you underground and I'll never see you again!"

"What are you talking about Toby?" asked Rosie feeling sorry for the man trapped in a boy's mind, but Toby was too upset to question him any further, so she decided to turn around and head back to the house. Toby didn't sleep very well that night; he was busy watching the bony people wandering aimlessly around the waste disposal site, their ghostly skeleton frames silhouetted in the moonlight.

Bob Martin, Ted Rogers and Andy McNeal operated the anaerobic digester. Most of the plant was fully automated. Once the waste lorries had pumped the slurry into the digester then it only needed one person to operate the entire process from the comfort of the control room. So the three men did an eight hour shift each, ensuring that the plant was operating twenty four hours a day, seven days a week. The plant had only been operating a few days when Bob, who was on the 10pm to 6am shift, noticed the pressure on one of the safety valves was above the danger level. It was 2 am and Ted was not due in for another 4 hours, so Bob had to investigate what had gone wrong on his own. The valves themselves were in the underground storage tank chamber that Keith and his men had hurriedly built. There was a three feet wide passageway that led around the entire tank. This was to ensure there was easy access for any maintenance or inspection of the tank. The only access to the underground chamber was a trap door in the steel floor. A metal ladder then dropped to the concrete floor below. The whole room was lit by 8 large florescent light tubes which gave ample light to the huge room.

Bob slid the bolt on the trap door and pulled it open. He then climbed down the ladder and switched the lights on. Everything looked fine on the ladder side, but as Bob stepped around the first corner, he saw that part of the retaining wall had collapsed on to the tank. It had blocked the passageway, so it was impossible to see if the tank had been damaged. Bob noticed a slight smell of methane lingering in the passageway, but he couldn't see if the safety valve had been damaged because it was buried. Suddenly the steel door slammed shut and he heard the bolt slide across, locking him in. Bob looked at his watch. It was nearly three in the morning, had Ted crept up and closed the hatch on him for a joke? Bob climbed the ladder and started banging on the trap door.

"Come on, Ted, let me out, you've had your little joke. Now let me out!"

There was no answer. So he banged again, and then listened; he thought he heard a scratching sound coming from the other side of the tank. He climbed back down the ladder and went to investigate. One of the overhead fluorescent tubes started flickering, then suddenly shattered, spraying him with glass. All the other lights immediately went out. Bob felt very afraid. He fumbled around in his pocket for his mobile phone. He hated the dark, and the scratching noise had started again, only this time it was louder. His hand gripped his mobile and he quickly switched on the torch light, it wasn't very bright and then he remembered he had been going to charge the battery as soon as he came into work. He dialled Ted's number but there was no dialling tone, and then he thought perhaps down here there was no signal. Bob's imagination began to take over; he could still hear the scratching noises. His mobile shone a small beam of light so he was able to see where he was treading.

He began to shuffle back around the tank to where the wall had collapsed. He could just see the earth behind the wall moving slightly; perhaps the wall was still collapsing. As he moved a little closer suddenly a bony hand gripped his ankle and pulled him over. He fell to the floor and dropped his phone. More hands gripped him and he could feel himself being pulled underground. He kicked and struggled, he could see his mobile illuminating a small area in front of him. He reached out to pick it up, but a bony foot trod on his hand. He looked up to see a tall skeletal figure standing over him. He grabbed the skeleton's ankle with his other hand and yanked at it, sending it crashing to the ground. It smashed into a hundred pieces on the concrete floor. He was still being dragged underground; there were too many bony hands pulling at him only his arms were free. He stuck his arms out to stop himself being sucked further into the ground. His torch was slowly becoming further and further away. Bob looked at the dimming torch for the last time before he was dragged underground.

When Ted arrived the next morning at 5.45 am he went into the unlocked control room, but Bob was not there. He shouted out, but there was no response. Everything was eerily quiet. He went outside and walked around the site looking for Bob. He then checked the toilets, but there was no sign of him. Ted went back inside to the control room and sat down, He was wondering why Bob had left the site unattended when he noticed the safety valve red warning light was flashing. He rushed down to the storage tank, slid the bolt on the trap door and opened it. A strong smell of methane gas rose into the air as, without thinking, Ted switched on the lights.

Suddenly a spark from the broken fluorescent light ignited the gas. Ted was killed instantly by the explosion as the whole underground tank erupted into a ball of fire, shattering all the windows in the house across the road.

Toby had been watching the site from his window to see if the bony people were still there. Suddenly the glass shattered and he was thrown across the room by the force of the explosion. He lay there dazed, his face covered in blood from the shattering glass. He started to cry, then felt the strong arms of Rosie around him lifting him to his feet. She pulled some of the glass fragments from his face and bathed it in warm water. Ambulances and fire engines arrived shortly afterwards and treated most of the patients with cuts and bruises.

By the time that the Fire Brigade finally had the blaze under control much of the anaerobic digester had been destroyed, along with three of the four fermenting tanks. But the biggest shock was the discovery of thousands of human bones scattered over the site. After the official investigation into the cause of the explosion and the four deaths and one missing person, the site was cleared. All the human bones were collected and buried in a corner of the site with a dignified church service. The whole site was transformed into a quiet sanctuary where people could walk along the grass paths and admire the beauty of the surrounding area. There were two memorials erected: one to the four men who lost their lives erecting the anaerobic digester; and the other to the unknown inhabitants of the Roman town buried on this site.

Toby still stands to this day looking out of his top floor window over the newly planted trees and flowers. Grass paths now wind their way between the park benches, people take their dogs for walks and sometimes stop to read the inscriptions on the memorial stones. Toby never saw any more bony people, now they had been laid to rest, but he never ever ventured into the sanctuary.

PROFESSOR LANSBURY'S DOG

CHAPTER 1

Professor Alan Lansbury was a leading brain surgeon who had received an OBE for his pioneering research on the human brain. In the last ten years he had treated and removed over one hundred brain tumours. He had also operated on car crash victims who had very little chance of survival, with an 80 % success rate. His team of young trainees worshipped the ground he walked on; to them he was a god.

But there was a dark side to Professor Lansbury. Unbeknown to his trainees the Professor was experimenting with stem cells and had injected some of the brain damaged patients, to see if the stem cells could repair the damaged part of their brains. He had some success, but most patients had rejected the implants and died. Two had survived for over a year, but were still severely brain damaged, so he was reluctant to tell anybody about his experiments.

He had been happily married to his wife Gillian, for over thirty years. They lived in a small village in Oxfordshire, in a pretty three bedroom house with a large garden. Their two children were both married and had moved away from the area. The Professor was a quiet man, but very generous and often donated large sums of money to various charities, so he had become quite well known, often appearing on television and chat shows. Gillian, however, was becoming bored with their lifestyle. She was nearly 10 years younger than her husband and wanted to travel abroad and see some excitement before she got too old. Alan was away all day and got home late, so she had joined the local parish council and had immersed herself in the village life, organizing fetes, jumble sales and coffee mornings, but she was still very lonely and did not have many friends.

The Professor worked up in London at the University College Hospital's Brain Trauma Unit. Most weekdays his wife would drive him to Didcot Parkway Train Station, where he would catch the 7.30 am express up to Paddington Station. He then took the tube to the Edgeware Road, from where it was just a short walk to the hospital. The whole journey took just over one hour, so when he returned home he was pretty tired.

As he was getting into bed one evening and was just falling asleep. Gillian whispered in his ear. "Now the children have all left and you are away all day, can I have a dog?"

Alan was so tired he murmured," Yes, I suppose so," and then dozed off into a deep sleep. The next morning Gillian was up bright and early. She shouted up to Alan, "Hurry up, breakfast is on the table!" Alan stumbled down the stairs and sat down, still half asleep.

"Here's a nice cup of tea, this will wake you up," Gillian said. After a long pause, she continued, "Could I go down to the Rescue Centre and see if there are any suitable dogs available?" Alan looked up as he was just about to eat his bacon and eggs.

"I don't remember anything about a dog," he said.

"But I asked you last night and you said I could have one," Gillian moaned. Alan looked at his watch: it was 7am and they would have to leave soon. He did not want to start an argument, so he reluctantly agreed. After Gillian had dropped Alan off at the train station she hurried back home and by 9am she was at the Rescue Centre. She asked the receptionist if any dogs were available for adoption and after filling out some forms Gillian was shown along rows of kennels, each with a different dog curled up inside. As she passed the tenth kennel she noticed a Black Labrador sitting on its hind legs in a begging position.

"That's a nice dog," she said.

The kennel maid told Gillian that the dog was approximately 2 years old and they had called her Lady because she had such a gentle nature. She had been abandoned and left tied up to the front door of the Rescue Centre. After a long discussion with the receptionist it was decided Gillian could take Lady home on a month's trial.

That evening when Alan opened the front door he was surprised to see a large black dog sitting in the hall looking at him. Lady got to her feet, went up to Alan and licked his hand.

"She seems very well-behaved," said Alan. "What's her name?" After Gillian had told him all about Lady, he quickly became very attached to the dog. By the time the month's trial had ended, Alan and Lady had become inseparable.

CHAPTER 2

Things were going well at the hospital. Professor Lansbury had in the last few days made amazing progress with the Stem Cell Programme. A young lad of fifteen had been brought to his operating theatre. He had been knocked over by a speeding car and had suffered severe head injuries. He was admitted as a DOA (Dead on Arrival), so the Professor had connected the lad to a life support machine and after a few jolts with the defibrillator had managed to restart his heart. Although the lad was stabilized, he was still in an induced coma. It was getting late and the Professor wanted to go home.

"The boy is stable now," said the Professor to his colleagues. "I think we will look at him tomorrow and decide what to do next."

After a tiring journey he finally got home at 7.30pm to find his best friend waiting for him by the front door. "Hello Lady," he said as he took off his coat. "What have you been up to today?" The dog got up and licked Alan's hand, her tail wagging furiously and followed him into the kitchen. Gillian was busy getting the evening meal out of the oven. "You're late," she said. "I waited at the station for over 30 minutes."

"I'm sorry," said Alan. "We had a DOA brought in today, so had to stabilize him before I came home. I got a taxi back from the station." During their evening meal Alan told Gillian all about the young lad.

"You work too hard, you should be taking things a little easier now," said Gillian. "Why can't you get your colleagues to do some of your work?" Alan was feeling tired and did not answer, he had heard it all before and hated being nagged.

"I am going for a lie down" he said and went upstairs to his bedroom, with the dog following.

"Now, you know you should not be in here, Lady," said Alan.

He looked into the dog's eyes and knew what the dog was thinking. "You are not sleeping in here tonight" said Alan. Lady got up and left the room, but a few minutes later had returned with a blanket in her mouth. She dropped the blanket at his feet, and looked at her master with big sorrowful eyes.

"Oh, come on then" Alan said. "But you'd better not let my wife catch you!"

Lady unravelled her blanket and put it at the side of the bed, then curled up beside her master. As Alan lay on his bed he marvelled at how intelligent Lady was. It seemed as if the dog could read his lips. His thoughts went back to the young lad at the hospital and what he was going to do to save the boy's life. With his brain working overtime he slowly drifted into a deep sleep.

The next morning Alan woke with a start, he quickly looked at his watch it was 6.50am then he remembered Lady, he looked down the side of the bed but the dog and her blanket had gone. He quickly had a wash, got dressed and rushed downstairs, expecting Gillian to start moaning about the dog sleeping in his bedroom, but Gillian was in a good mood.

"Good morning dear, she said as he sat down at the breakfast table, "did you have a good night's sleep?"

"Yes, thanks, but where's Lady?" said Alan looking around.

"She's still sound asleep in her bed, why do ask?" said Gillian. Alan mumbled some excuse and remarked they would have to leave soon, or he would miss the 7.30 train. He went and said his goodbyes to Lady and winked at her as he and his wife left for the station.

When he arrived at the hospital he quickly got changed and went to see the young lad. Two of his colleagues, Brian Benson and Thomas Granger were already there, eager to see what the Professor had planned. He explained that he was going to put the lad through a brain scanner to see if they could spot the damaged part of the brain, then open up the skull and freeze the brain before injecting the stem cells. This he hoped would give the stem cells time to attach before the body could reject them. The Professor looked around at his two colleagues.

"You realise what we are about to do is totally illegal?" he said. "We are experimenting with this lad's life. If he lives we will be heroes, but if he dies we could be accused of murder. We must keep this to ourselves and not tell anyone, do you both agree?"

Both his colleagues nodded and agreed. They quickly put the lad through the brain scanner, and then looked at the negatives. The Professor spotted the damage straight away. "We will take him down to the operating theatre and start the procedure immediately."

As the boy lay on the operating table they shaved his head and marked where the skull had to be opened. The Professor cut along the lines and peeled away the skin to reveal the skull. Using the special bone saw, he gently cut into the skull and removed a section to expose the brain. His colleagues then inserted a tiny freezing rod into the cerebrospinal fluid surrounding the brain, and as the fluid began to cool the Professor injected the stem cells directly into the damaged part of the brain.

"We will keep the brain just above freezing until tomorrow. Then we can see if there is any change in the brain pattern," said the Professor. "Until then I want you to examine the blood vessels surrounding the damaged part of the brain and make sure they are not bleeding. When the trainees come in later you can teach them all about stem cells. I have a meeting with the board of directors in half an hour, so I must leave now." The Professor changed his clothes, put on his coat and left the hospital.

The next morning the Professor met his colleague in the operating theatre. After removing the freezing rod and letting the cerebrospinal fluid reach its normal temperature, they connected electrodes to various parts of the brain to see if there were any changes.

"The graph shows there is some brain activity" said Brian. "But I can't say whether it's from the damaged part."

"Good," said the Professor," at least we can bring him out of the induced coma, that should give us a good indication as to whether he will be brain damaged or not." As the boy slowly recovered, the graph which was still connected suddenly began to show bursts of energy.

"Well, there's certainly life there," said the Professor. Thomas and Brian went to shake hands and congratulate him, but the Professor said: "It's too early to celebrate yet, let's wait until the boy's conscious."

It was two days before he had recovered enough to be able to talk. The lad's name was George Davidson, he could not remember anything about the accident, but told the Professor he still had a slight headache. The Professor explained about the operation and said the headaches were due to the bruising and would get better in a few days, meanwhile he would give him some drugs to ease the pain.

A week later, George Davidson had recovered fully and had no lasting brain damage. The newspapers printed a whole page about the revolutionary operation. The Professor had to make more television appearances and magazines wanted exclusive interviews about his family life. It all became very tiring and he was glad to get home to a quiet life.

CHAPTER 3

Over the next few weeks, life carried on as normal in the Lansbury household. Gillian had been a lot happier since Lady had arrived and had taken the dog for long walks every afternoon. She had met lots of people and had made some new friends. She looked forward to the weekends when Alan joined her and they both took the dog for walks, stopping at various village pubs for a light lunch and a beer. But one Saturday morning things did not go as planned. Alan and Gillian were in the garden sitting in the sun, with Lady at their feet fast asleep. Alan decided to unlock the car which was parked at the side of the road just outside the garden. Lady got up and followed her master. As he opened the gate the dog saw a cat and immediately gave chase. Before he could stop her, Lady ran straight in front of a car coming around the corner. The car driver swerved and stamped on the brakes, but it was too late. The car's front bumper hit the dog and she was bowled over. She lay at the side of the road, not moving. The driver got out of his car just as Alan reached his beloved dog.

The shocked driver apologized and said: "The dog ran straight out in front of me! There was nothing I could have done." Alan picked up his dog, without looking at the driver. Gillian came through the garden gate.

"Oh no, what's happened?" she said. Alan did not answer for a while. He tried to hold back the tears, but could not. After he had recovered enough to speak, he said: "Quick open up the car's tailgate! Lady's been knocked over. I'll take her to the vet's at Wallingford." Alan put the dog gently down in the back of the car. Blood was coming from the dog's mouth and ear. They both got in the car and sped off, leaving the other driver bewildered at the side of the road.

Alan only took five minutes to get to the vet's. Gillian ran ahead and opened the door. Mary, the vet, was at the reception desk, she was a long standing friend of the Professor.

"Quick, bring the dog in here," she said, pointing to the operating table. Alan laid the dog down on the table.

"She's been knocked over by a car," he said, tears still rolling down his cheeks. After a quick examination the vet told Alan that the dog was haemorrhaging and the kindest thing was to put her down.

"No, you can't do that!" cried Alan. "You haven't even tried to save her."

"I can assure you there's nothing we can do," said Mary.

"You might not be able to do anything" said Alan. "But I can!" He picked the dog up and rushed out to his car, his wife following close behind him.

"What are you going to do?" Gillian asked as she climbed into the car, Alan was oblivious to what she had said. He was on his mobile phone, talking to his colleagues at the hospital.

"Meet me in the operating theatre in 1 hour, we have an emergency!" he said. He looked across at his wife. "Are you coming?" She nodded. He put his foot hard down on the accelerator and sped off to the hospital.

The traffic up to London was not as bad as he had feared and they made good progress. He parked outside the hospital in his reserved parking space, rushed inside the private entrance to the Trauma Unit and a few minutes later came out with a trolleyed stretcher. Gillian helped Alan lift the lifeless dog onto the stretcher and covered the dog with a sheet. They wheeled the stretcher in to the operating theatre where Thomas and Brian were already waiting. Alan told Gillian to wait in the reception area until they had finished She reluctantly agreed and went back down the corridor. Alan lifted the sheet from the stretcher and both Thomas and Brian's mouths dropped open. They stared at the dog and then back at the Professor.

"You don't expect us to operate on an animal, do you?" said Brian. The Professor explained about his beloved dog, Lady, how she had the same injuries as George Davidson, the boy they had operated on two weeks ago.

"Why can't we do the same operation on my dog?" he demanded.

"But the boy is a human being," protested Brian. "This is just an animal!"

"Not just any animal, said the Professor. "She's very intelligent and I will do anything to save her. Will you help me, please?" Brian and Thomas looked at each other and then back at the Professor's tearstained face and both nodded.

"We will go through the same procedures as we did with the boy" said the Professor. He paused "But we will inject some of the boy's stem cells into the dog's brain."

Thomas and Brian were both shocked. Thomas spoke first.

"But Professor, you are meddling with nature!" Then Brian interrupted, "If you go ahead with this and it's a success, you will have created an abomination"

The Professor pleaded with his colleagues to give the dog a chance, promising to euthanize Lady himself if the operation did not go as planned. They both reluctantly agreed, and prepared the dog for the operation. All went well until they exposed the brain. It was badly swollen and pushing against the skull. After they had stopped the bleeding and injected the human stem cells, the Professor suggested they make the skull slightly bigger so it did not irritate the brain tissues. as they grew. The operation took nearly two hours. The dog did look a bit peculiar with a raised cranium and no hair. But the Professor was happy. He wheeled the dog along to a private room and left her on the stretcher with all the drips and breathing tubes still connected, he then locked the door and returned to his two colleagues.

"All we can do now is wait and see," he said. "If she survives for the next 24 hours, she has a good chance of a complete recovery". The Professor asked his colleagues to keep the operation a complete secret, as they all knew they would be struck off the medical register and possibly face a jail sentence for the misuse of hospital equipment.

CHAPTER 4

On Monday morning the Professor checked on Lady as soon as he arrived at the hospital. He had driven up in his car just in case she had improved, and he could then take her home. But there was no change; she had a good heartbeat and the EEG machine showed that the brain's electrical activity was improving. Thomas caught the Professor just as he was leaving the ward and about to lock the door.

"We have a problem," said Thomas. "We had a phone call just before you arrived from Sir Michael French, head of the Board of Directors. After your success with George Davidson, they are all visiting us today at 10 o'clock to look around our facilities, and he wants you to show them around." Thomas paused for a moment, "What are we going to do about the dog?"

"Let me worry about that" said the Professor "as long as the dog doesn't wake up, I think we'll be OK." When the directors came into the Trauma Unit, led by Sir Michael French, Professor Lansbury was there to greet them.

Sir Michael French spoke first, "I hope this is not an inconvenience to you at short notice, but after your success with the Davidson lad we decided to increase your budget for your research and would like a look around the unit, if that's alright with you?"

"That's no problem" said the Professor "follow me." He showed them around the operating theatre, the pretreatment rooms, the recovery rooms and the private wards. One of the directors tried the door of the room that Lady was in.

"Why is this door locked?" he asked. The Professor was stumped for a minute, until Brian said "We have a water leak, sir, and are waiting for the plumber to fix it. It's a safety precaution

"Good thinking" said Sir Michael. "We don't want any accidents and then people suing us, do we?" The directors seemed satisfied with what they had seen. They all shook hands with the Professor, congratulating him on his success and then left. When they had gone Thomas said, "I think we ought to move that dog as soon as it wakes up."

The Professor agreed as he did not want to get his colleagues into trouble, after all they had other operations to do so would need the ward. That evening Lady opened her eyes and though she was still very drowsy, it was decided to move her that night. The Professor covered the semiconscious dog with a sheet and pushed the trolley to the private entrance. While his colleagues kept a lookout, he gently slid the stretcher into the back of his estate car, keeping the drips and breathing apparatus attached, and then drove as carefully as he could back home. His wife was waiting at the front door as he pulled up. He asked Gillian to help him with the stretcher. They placed the stretcher on a camp bed that Gillian had earlier put in the lounge.

"She should be fine now," Alan said. "I will just go and lock the car." When he came back Lady was fully awake and tried to get up.

"I'll sleep down here tonight," said Alan, "just to comfort her."

Gillian went off to the kitchen to make her husband some supper, but when she returned with a plate full of sandwiches, Alan and the dog were fast asleep. She decided not to wake them, left the sandwiches on the table and closed the door behind her. The next day Alan called the hospital saying he had 'flu and needed a few days off, but truthfully he wanted to make sure his dog was fully recovered before he went back to work. Over the next few days Lady made a remarkable recovery, they even took her for a long walk up Wittenham Clumps, a local beauty spot. On the Monday morning when Alan went back to work, Lady seemed to be her normal self again, or so they thought.

Over the next few weeks great changes were being made at the hospital. The Board of Directors had increased the Professor's budget by a substantial amount. One of the preparation rooms was to be converted into another operating theatre. Thomas and Brian had been promoted and two trainees had been upgraded to personal assistants to work alongside them, although the Professor was still overseeing operations. They had also been allocated two of the latest portable EEG machines and two eye tracking devices that interacted with a computer, adapted specially for stroke victims that had been paralyzed. This especially pleased the Professor, as now he did not have to work such long hours and could leave a lot earlier. The unit's workload had increased though, now they were taking in severe stroke victims that had been left brain damaged. In the last week alone they had treated seven patients. It was the last patient, Adam Charlton, that the Professor was most interested in.

He was 70 years old and had been brought in completely paralyzed after having suffered a severe stroke. When he was connected to the EEG machine, however, it showed his brain was still working normally. The Professor decided to try out the eye tracking device which was connected to a word processing program. He said "Mr. Charlton, I know you can hear me. Blink once for yes and twice for no. Are you in pain?" When the monitor showed the word: no, he looked at Brian who had joined them.

"That's amazing," said Brian. "Can he understand everything you ask him?"

"Yes, I think he can," said the Professor . . ."And with the eye tracking device he'll be able to talk to us through the computer by blinking his eyes."

The Professor then asked him, "Do you want a drink?" They both looked at the monitor, where letters began to appear and form words: "Yes, a cup of tea."

Brian went to the staff kitchen and a few minutes later returned with a cup of tea. They had to feed the patient through a tube directly into his stomach as the only muscles he could move were around his eyes. The Professor and Brian talked to Adam Charlton for some time before he became tired and wanted to sleep. That afternoon on his way home the Professor had a brilliant idea: he would buy an MRI machine, an EEG machine and the Eye Tracking Device and connect them to his dog to see what would happen. He could afford it and if it did not work he would donate the machines to another hospital. When he got home he told his wife what he was going to do.

"You must be mad!" she said. "Why waste all that money on a stupid idea like that?"

"But don't you see," said Alan. "I could be the first person to have a conversation with an animal!"

"I still think it's a silly idea," said Gillian and stormed off into the garden. Alan looked across at his dog who had been sitting looking at him since he came in.

"Come on girl, I'll take you for a walk." As he got up, the dog ran into the kitchen and came back with a lead in her mouth.

"I am sure you can read my lips," he said as he connected the lead to Lady's collar. They left through the front door, avoiding his wife in the garden.

CHAPTER 5

The next day the Professor discussed his idea with Brian. He trusted him and knew he would not tell anybody. Brian thought the Professor was becoming a little eccentric, but did not say anything. The Professor ordered the machines through the hospital, explaining it was for a donation to another hospital and that he would pay for them. A few days later the equipment arrived at his house. The Professor was excited and could not wait to get home; Brian was treating another stroke victim with severe brain damage. They used the same treatment as before, freezing then injecting stem cells directly into the damaged part of the brain. The Professor helped Brian with the injections, and then left him to finish off.

He now found it more convenient to drive to the hospital as he was working fewer hours and was able to get home a lot earlier. He arrived home at 4.15 pm and while his wife was busy in the garden, he set up all the equipment in his study. When Gillian shouted that his dinner was on the table, he left what he was doing and went through to the kitchen.

"You were home early," she said. "What have you been doing?"

He did not want to tell her, but thought she was going to find out anyway, so he blurted out: "I am setting some machines up for Lady. I am going to test my theory to see if it works."

"And I will see if you have wasted our money!" she replied rather sharply. After they had finished dinner, Alan hurried off to his study. Lady was already in there, eager to see what her master had brought home. He sat the dog down and connected the probes to her head, then switched on all the machines. He looked directly into her eyes and said "What is your name?"

He looked at the monitor, but it remained blank. The EEG machine, however, was going crazy recording the brain's electrical activity. His wife walked in and sat down in the armchair, he tried again.

"Can you read my lips?" He looked around at his wife and then back at the monitor; the screen was still blank. Gillian was about to say I told you so, when Alan said, "Oh, how stupid I am! Of course Lady can't blink the answers on to the monitor because she has never been taught the alphabet."

He asked Gillian if they still had their children's primary school books. His wife replied "All the children's stuff is packed away in boxes in the attic." He quickly went upstairs, dropped the loft ladder and climbed into the attic. Five minutes later he returned beaming from ear to ear, he had found three alphabet books and a few toys.

"Now let's see if this makes a difference," he said. He opened the first book, pointed at the letter A and mouthed the letter to Lady. After a few seconds the letter A appeared on the monitor.

"It works!" he shouted, looking at his wife in triumph. "All I have to do now is teach her the rest of the alphabet." His wife got up and went back into the garden; she hated it when her husband proved he was right and she was wrong.

Alan looked at his dog and said, "Lady you have a lot of learning to do, starting from now!"

After four hours his dog had learned the whole alphabet. Alan could not wait to tell his colleagues at the hospital the next day. When he finally went to bed that night his brain was busy thinking what to teach the dog next. When he arrived at work the next morning, he immediately called Brian and

Thomas into his office, he could hardly contain himself when the two men came in and sat down.

"I've done it!" he blurted out. Brian and Thomas looked at each other, wondering what an earth he was talking about. The Professor continued, "I've taught my dog the alphabet."

"That's impossible," said Thomas. "She still has a dog's brain."

"But it's true," insisted the Professor.

Brian interrupted "We injected the dog with human stem cells, right? What if the cells have grown and somehow taken over the rest of the brain?"

"That's highly unlikely," said Thomas. They continued to argue, but could not come up with any rational answer other than it was a fluke of nature.

Over the next month Alan taught the dog to connect letters to make words, only simple words such as cat, dog, mat etc. But it was a start and the dog seemed keen to learn. Alan then taught the dog to read by showing her starter books for young children, he would open the page and mouth the words and point to the picture. It was slowgoing having to connect all the machines together before they could start, so he designed a skull cap that was already wired to the machines and all he had to do was place it on the dog's head

A month later, Alan could ask the dog a simple question, and as long as he was in front of her and Lady could read his lips, she would blink her eyes and the answer would appear on the monitor.

He spent hours every evening after work teaching the dog more and more. Lady could now recognize numbers and ask questions herself through the monitor. Alan was spending more time at home and only went up to the hospital two or three days a week. Brian and Thomas always enquired how the dog was getting on, but the Professor usually changed the subject. So, in the end, the dog was never mentioned.

CHAPTER 6

A year went by and the Professor had taken early retirement. He had been given a golden handshake, but he still visited the hospital occasionally just to see how Brian and Thomas were managing. He used to spend a lot of time in his office having conservations with his dog; in fact he spent more time talking to Lady than he did his wife.

It was one sunny morning in July, a day he would remember for the rest of his life. The Professor had got up early and taken Lady for a walk. He liked to go early to avoid other dog walkers as they always asked the same questions: "What happened to your dog's head?" Or, "Why is your dog's head shaped like that?" He usually told them she was deformed at birth and the reply was always "Oh the poor thing."

When Alan got back from his walk at 7.30 am, Gillian had cooked him a breakfast of bacon and eggs. He sat down and started eating his meal. His wife asked if he would like to come shopping with her. But he hated trudging around the shops not knowing what his wife wanted, trying a dress on then asking him what he thought of it. Then, when he told her he did not like it, she would say he was old fashioned, so he declined the offer.

"I suppose you are going to spend all day talking to that bloody dog?" she asked mockingly. Alan could see this leading to another argument and he could feel a headache coming on, so he said, "No, as a matter of fact I am driving up to the hospital to see Brian and Thomas, if that's all right?"

"You do what you like," Gillian said. "But don't forget your dental appointment." She then stormed off into the garden.

Alan finished his cup of tea, then went and said goodbye to his dog. He got in his car and started his journey up to London.

When he arrived at the hospital, his head was throbbing so badly he went straight to his office and took a couple of painkillers. He lay back in his reclining office chair, closed his eyes and gradually drifted off to sleep. He woke suddenly, looked at his watch and saw it was quarter past one. Then he remembered the dentist's appointment at half past two. If he left now, he thought, he would just make it. He ran out of the office, got in his car and sped off and did not even have time to sit down before the receptionist called his name. After he had his teeth checked and cleaned he left the dentist. At 3 o'clock he was back in his car on his way home. When he arrived, he immediately knew something was wrong: where was his dog? She always greeted him when he came home. He called her name, then listened, but could hear nothing.

Alan went into the office expecting Lady to be curled up in her bed fast asleep, but it was empty. He called out his wife's name, but there was no reply. He guessed she was still out shopping. He went into the kitchen and there in the corner was Lady. She did not move, and when he went over to her, he felt something warm and wet. Blood was oozing out of her side. He panicked, picked the dog up put her in the back of the car and rushed her to the vet's at Wallingford. Mary, the vet, was just cleaning out the treatment room when Alan rushed in with the dog in his arms.

"Quick!" he cried. "My dog's bleeding!" He put the dog on the operating table so Mary could examine her. Mary parted the fur around her lower stomach. "She's been shot," she said. "The bullet has passed right through her body, but it does not look like it has hit any vital organs."

"Will she be alright?" Alan asked.

"Well, she's still unconscious, probably through shock," Mary replied. "But she should make a full recovery. I will stitch the wounds and give her some antibiotics." As she was finishing, the dog began to come round. Mary asked "Is this the same dog you brought in last year with the brain haemorrhage?"

Alan did not know what to say at first, so he replied "Yes, we did a brain scan on her and managed to stop the bleeding."

Mary looked at him unbelievingly. "Well," she said, "after I examined her she seemed nearly dead to me. It must be some sort of miracle."

"Yes, I suppose it was," said Alan, not wanting to reveal any more. He thanked Mary, made an excuse that he must get home and asked if she could send him the bill. When Alan finally got home, he lifted his dog out of the car, took her inside and laid her on her bed. She was fully awake now, but very weak, so he decided to question her in the morning after she'd had a good rest. He went into the kitchen and looked at the wall clock; it was nearly 5 o' clock and his wife was still not home. He made himself some beans on toast and a mug of tea then sat down at the kitchen table and ate the meal. He kept looking at the clock, he decided if Gillian was not home by 6 o' clock he would start phoning her friends. Maybe her car had broken down, he thought, but why hadn't she rung him on her mobile?

He looked around the kitchen and then spotted her mobile phone on the shelf over the cooking range. He got up and went to the garage: Gillian's car was still there. Alan began to panic and then thought to himself: she's an independent woman and probably out with her friends, she will come home when she wants to. He calmed himself down with a nice cold beer from the fridge and sat down in the lounge. He switched on the television, went and got another beer, then lay down on the sofa and watched the evening news. Within thirty minutes he was sound asleep.

CHAPTER 7

He woke when something rough licked his face. He opened his eyes and looked at his watch; it was six o'clock in the morning, he had slept all night. Lady was sitting beside him, looking into his eyes. Alan then remembered his wife. He called her name, but there was no reply. He went to the kitchen and after a quick wash and a cup of tea, he began to think more clearly. His dog came into the kitchen, sniffed around and picked up a piece of paper and brought it over to Alan.

"What have you got there?" Alan asked her. He took the paper from her mouth and unfolded it. In bold capital letters was written:

WE HAVE TAKEN YOUR WIFE HOSTAGE SHE WILL NOT BE HARMED IF YOU PAY£1,000,000 FOR HER RELEASE. WE WILL RING YOU LATER FOR FURTHER INSTRUCTIONS. DO NOT CONTACT THE POLICE OR YOU WILL NEVER SEE YOUR WIFE AGAIN.

Alan sat staring at the letter until his dog nuzzled his hand. He looked at her and knew she wanted to tell him something. He got up and went into his office with the dog following behind. He put the skull cap on her head and switched on the machines. Alan looked into Lady's eyes and asked her if she knew what had happened to Gillian. After a few seconds, one word appeared on the monitor: Yes.

After questioning the dog for over an hour Alan began to understand. Just after he had left to go to the hospital, a van had pulled up outside the house. Two men knocked on the front door and when Gillian answered it, they had pushed their way in. One of the men grabbed Gillian, while the other put a sack over her head and tied her hands. She had screamed and when Lady attacked and bit one of the men, the other man kicked the dog off, pulled a gun and shot Lady. As they bundled Gillian in the side door of the van and drove off, Lady had dragged herself over to the window and had seen the number plate. It was TIL 8628. She had also remembered that the men were not English and spoke in a funny accent, and one had a black beard, but she had recognised three words HOMMER, SMIT and GARAGE.

Alan did not hesitate. As soon as he had written down all the information he rang the police. He was told not to touch anything and wait. It was not long before a police car arrived, two plain clothed officers knocked on the front door. When Alan opened it, the officers held up their ID cards. The man in front spoke first.

"I am Inspector Newman, and this is my assistant Sergeant Woods."

Alan invited them in and showed them the information he had written down.

"Where were you when all this was happening?" asked the Inspector.

"I was on my way up to the College Hospital in London," replied Alan."

"Then how did you obtain this information?" asked Inspector Newman. Alan hesitated for a moment, not knowing what to say.

"From my dog," said Alan, feeling a little uncomfortable. Inspector Newman leaned over to Alan and rather angrily said, "Professor Lansbury, if you have brought us out here on a wild goose chase, then I will arrest you for wasting police time."

"No, listen," said Alan. "My dog is very intelligent and I have taught her to lip read. We can communicate through a computer monitor. I can show you if like." He got up and went to the office, the two policemen followed him. His dog was lying in her bed.

"Come on, Lady," said Alan. "These gentlemen would like a demonstration of your talents." He put the skull cap on the dog's head and, with all the probes connected, switched on the machines.

"Now stand in front of the dog and ask her a question," said Alan. The Inspector looked at his colleague, who had a large grin on his face, but turned and spoke to the dog very slowly.

"Did you see the two men?" After a few minutes a single word appeared on the monitor: "Yes."

The Inspector at first thought it was a joke, so asked another question. "Can you describe the men?"

Again a sentence appeared on the monitor. As the Inspector questioned the dog more, Sergeant Woods was taking notes. After an hour they had quite a good idea what the men looked like, which coincided with what the Professor had already told them.

"Can I bring over some mug shots of suspected criminals who fit that description?" Inspector Newman asked. It was agreed that the two policemen would visit the next morning. They left after asking the Professor to stay in contact in case he thought of anything else.

The next morning there was a phone call. When Alan picked the phone up a deep foreign voice said, "You disobeyed me and informed the police, for that the ransom price has gone up to two million."

Then the phone went dead. Alan sat down, shocked. He could feel the tears welling up in his eyes. A knock on the front door brought him back to his senses. It was Inspector

Newman and Sergeant Woods. Alan quickly told them about the phone call, they then showed the book of photographs to Lady, when Alan had connected all the equipment up. The inspector slowly turned the pages until the word: STOP appeared on the monitor, and then another word appeared: HIM

Inspector Newman looked at the picture it was Abdul Maheen a known terrorist living in London. Inspector Newman looked pleased. They continued turning the pages until the end, but Lady did not see the man with the black beard, however Inspector Newman was satisfied with the result.

"We have also traced the van number," said the Inspector. "It was an Irish plate registered to Hammersmith Van Hire. We have contacted the Metropolitan Police who are investigating the company. I will fax them over this picture and see if it's the same man that hired the van."

The Inspector paused, flicked through his note pad and then said, "Just one other thing." He looked at the dog. "Could the words you remembered have been Hammer Smith instead of Hommer Smit?" He looked at the monitor, the reply was: Yes.

"OK," said the Inspector. "Sergeant Woods was a constable up in Hammersmith a few years ago. He told us there were some lockup garages under the Hammersmith Flyover which were owned and rented out by a Muslim Family. I think we ought to put the garages under surveillance and see if the man with the beard shows up. I will phone Chief Inspector Bradford of the Metropolitan Police and ask him to organize it." Both men shook hands with the Professor and then patted his dog on the head.

"You do have an amazing dog, Professor." said the Inspector. "Perhaps you should both work for us." Inspector

Newman laughed as he and Sergeant Woods left. "We'll keep you informed if we have any news" he said.

Late that night Alan received a phone call from the Inspector.

"We've found your wife, she's alive and well with just a few bruises to her arms but they are keeping her in hospital overnight just for a check-up. We have a few more questions to ask her, so will bring her back in the morning."

The next morning a police car pulled up outside Alan's house and out stepped Gillian. She ran into Alan's outstretched arms and he hugged her sobbing uncontrollably. "I'll let you have some time alone," said the Inspector. "Perhaps I can call around this afternoon?"

"That will be fine" said Gillian as she and her husband went indoors. Inspector Newman did go and see the Professor and his wife later that afternoon. He sat at the kitchen table and told them what had happened that day.

Chief Inspector Bradford had ordered two surveillance officers to watch the row of garages under the Hammersmith Flyover. Two were rented out by a tyre company. Two more were car repair and service garages. The fifth and sixth garages were a car spraying shop and the last two were empty. That evening a man with a black beard was seen entering the last garage with a bottle of water in his hand. He came out five minutes later without the bottle, locked the garage and walked off down the road. He was arrested and taken into custody and questioned. Later when officers broke into the garage they found it empty, apart from some old oil cans, a work bench and a lifting rig over a service pit. There were some heavy wooden planks covering the pit, when these were removed they found Gillian huddled in a corner. She had been tied around her hands and feet and gagged with gaffer tape.

"Then we took her to the hospital for a check-up," the Inspector continued. "I expect your wife has told you what happened. However, you will be glad to know the bearded man confessed. Apparently he got the idea for the kidnapping after seeing you on television, and hearing that you were wealthy. The gang thought the money could help support a terrorist network working in London. They're all under arrest now, thanks to your dog, Professor."

Alan patted Lady on the head, and said, "Yes, she is one in a million!"

The next morning, after a good night's sleep, Professor Lansbury and his wife Gillian were woken by loud talking outside their house. Gillian got up and went to the window; she pulled back the curtains, and quickly closed them again.

"Oh my God!" she said looking at her husband who had just sat up in bed. "There are loads of people outside with cameras." Alan got up and put his dressing gown on. He looked at his watch.

"It's only 8 o' clock in the morning," he said. "Can't anybody get a lie in around here?" He went over to the window, drew the curtains and opened the window. Immediately bulbs flashed and cameras whirled. Before he could say anything, the reporters shouted: "Can we have an interview?" and "Can we take a picture of your dog?" Alan closed the window and drew the curtain.

"What are we going to do?" asked Gillian. Alan thought for a moment: how had the press found out about Lady? Any of the policemen working with the Inspector could have informed the reporters about the case.

"I suppose I will have to make a statement," he said. He quickly had a wash, got dressed and went downstairs into the kitchen. By the time he had made a cup of tea Gillian had joined him. The crowd outside began knocking on the front door and one reporter even opened the letterbox and shouted.

"Professor Lansbury, please let us take a few photos and then we will leave you alone." After a few minutes the Professor and his wife opened the front door, again there was an immediate flashing of bulbs.

"Can we take some pictures of your dog?" the reporters all shouted at once. The Professor raised his arms, "Enough, enough!" he shouted. "You can't all come in. I will speak to six of you at a time." The reporters all surged forward. The Professor let six people in, then shut the door

"Right gentlemen, follow me." He led them into the office where Lady was sitting in her bed, wondering what all the noise was. It frightened her when the bulbs began flashing.

"Is this the talking dog?" said one reporter.

"Just one minute," said the Professor. "If you all quieten down I will answer your questions and then give you a demonstration. First of all, my dog can't talk." There was a muffled sigh from the reporters.

"But," he continued, "She can lip read and can communicate with her eyes through the computer monitor as I will now show you."

He connected the probes to all the machines and then put the skull cap on Lady's head.

"Now if you all stand back and look at the monitor," he paused. "I will need a volunteer." One reporter stuck his hand up.

"Right, stand in front of my dog and ask her a question." The reporter felt a bit silly and wished he had not volunteered. "Go on, ask her!" the Professor urged.

The reporter cleared his throat and said "Can you hear me?" Then they all looked at the monitor.

"Yes, I can hear you." The reporters were amazed, not expecting such a quick response.

"Ask something a bit more complicated," said the Professor "but one sentence at a time." The reporter thought for a moment and then said "Were you scared of the men that shot you?" Again they looked at the monitor.

"No, I wasn't scared. I wanted to hurt the men."

Well, that reply convinced the reporters that the dog was for real and they all wanted to talk to Lady. The Professor told them that would be enough for now as the other reporters wanted their interview. He showed them to the front door and then let the remaining reporters in.

After the last reporter had left, things returned to normal again. Alan and Gillian sat down and had a very late breakfast. Lady had joined them and was tucking into a bowl of the very best dog food. It was a beautiful day and they decided to take Lady for a walk. Over the last couple of days Alan had come to realise just how much he had missed his wife and was determined to change his ways. They were talking to each other more and more and for a while his dog had taken a back seat.

The next day most of the newspapers carried a front page story about 'The Amazing Labrador Identifies Kidnap Suspects', or 'The Wonder Dog solves Kidnap Ordeal.' One paper actually printed: 'Wonder Dog talks to Police about Kidnap Case.' Alan was horrified he read the whole article and found most of it was pure fabrication.

"After all I explained to them, they still can't get it right" he said. Gillian felt a bit sorry for him. "All the papers exaggerate, Alan," she said. "That's what sells them."

"I know," he said. "But I wish they would get the facts right!" he paused for a few minutes. "I know," he said, "let's go for a picnic up Streatley Hills, the walk will do us all good." Gillian agreed and set about making the sandwiches.

CHAPTER 8

It was about four years after the operation that Lady's eyesight began to deteriorate. The Professor noticed it when the dog blinked an answer on the monitor to one of his questions, some of the words did not make sense. And, more importantly, Lady's jaw had dropped to one side. He guessed her brain was still growing and was touching the optic nerve causing spasms of the face. He lay in bed that night thinking about what he was going to do, and then whispered to his wife

"Lady's in pain and if we do not release the pressure on the optic nerve, she will go blind."

"Can't you do another operation?" said Gillian.

"I'm afraid not" said the Professor. "We've already increased the skull size, but the brain has grown so much there's simply no more room for it to expand."

"What are you going to do?" asked Gillian.

"I simply don't know" said the Professor. "I will have to sleep on it." He said goodnight to Gillian, rolled over and pretended to go to sleep, but deep down he knew there was only one solution.

The next morning Lady did not want to go for a walk. She lay in her bed until 11 o' clock when finally she got, up had a drink of water and went into the garden. Alan noticed she was not very steady on her feet and had stumbled over the back door step. When the dog came back in, Alan looked at her.

"Do you want to tell me something Lady?" he said. Lady blinked once, he led her into the office and placed the skull cap on her head, then switched the machines on. He had to wait sometime before anything appeared on the monitor, even then a lot of words were spelt wrong and he had to guess most of it.

"My head hurts and I can't see properly," was written on the monitor.

Alan looked into the dog's eyes, he could see she was in a lot of pain and could feel himself welling up inside. With tears in his eyes he said. "Lady there is nothing more I can do, your brain is pressing on the optic nerve, that's why your eyesight is affected."

He waited for the reply on the monitor: "If you can't help me, then put me to sleep."

Alan could not contain his feelings anymore and burst into tears. He looked at his beloved dog. "I can't do it!" he sobbed, and between the tears he read another message.

"Please, stop this pain!" Alan went into the kitchen and opened the cupboard. He felt for a syringe he had hidden in a box on the back shelf. He took it out and went back into the office. Lady looked at him; her face was sunken on one side, as if she was having another spasm. Alan wiped away his tears, sat down next to his dog and pulled her onto his lap. He hugged the dog one more time then placed the syringe to the dog's neck and injected the morphine. He cradled her head and watched as Lady slowly closed her eyes. He sat there for ten minutes before his wife came into the office. She could see her husband was very upset, she knelt down and cuddled him.

"Let's go into the garden" she said. "Lady always lay under the apple tree when it was hot, we could bury her there."

Alan got up and with his dog in his arms followed his wife into the garden. He didn't say anything, but kept his emotions at bay. He put the dog down and started digging the grave. When he had finished, he lined the grave with Lady's old blanket then placed the dog in the grave. He suddenly ran back into the house and came out with the skull cap.

"We won't be needing this anymore" he said and placed the skull cap in the grave next to his dog. He then draped the blanket over the dog's body and filled in the hole. Gillian planted some daffodil bulbs on the grave when Alan had finished. They both stood looking at the grave until Gillian, broke the silence.

"Let's go inside and have a nice cup of tea," she said. "We can't do any more here." Alan didn't answer, but followed her into the house. He sat down at the kitchen table and buried his head in his hands.

CHAPTER 9

The Professor and his wife did not get another dog, despite being advised to do so by all their friends, Alan could not bear the heartache again if anything happened. It was two weeks before he ventured up to the hospital to see his old friends, Brian and Thomas, and tell them the sad news. They both felt sorry for the Professor, but partly relieved that the dog was dead

"Maybe that was for the best" said Brian "Lady had a good life and you gave her an extra four years, don't forget that."

"I know" said the Professor, "but there's a big empty space in my life now." Brian put his arm around the Professor's shoulder to comfort him.

"You could always come back to work with us" said Thomas

"Thanks, but no thanks" said the Professor. "I think my working days are over, but I will pop in now and again just to keep an eye on you." He shook their hands and said goodbye, walked out of the hospital, got in his car and started his journey home.

The Professor did not arrive home that afternoon. As he was driving through the London suburbs, a black Labrador dashed out of a driveway, straight in front of the Professor's car. He swerved to miss the dog and drove into the front of an oncoming lorry. His car was buried under the lorry's front axle. Alan did not feel any pain; he seemed to drift out of his car and float above the lorry.

He looked down on the mayhem below. The lorry had jack-knifed across the road, blocking it completely. A queue of vehicles had begun to build up and some of the car drivers had got out of their cars to see if they could help. The lorry driver stepped down from his cab. Alan heard him say.

"Quick, somebody phone for an ambulance, he may still be alive!" Another person said "I shouldn't think anybody would survive that."

A few minutes later the sirens of a police car, then a fire engine could be heard. The police quickly closed the road in both directions and put up diversion signs while the firemen got out their cutting equipment and began cutting away the front of the lorry.

Alan was completely oblivious that the man trapped under the lorry was himself. He looked on as they pulled the broken twisted body of a man from the wreckage. An ambulance pulled up, lights flashing and two paramedics jumped out and went over to the body.

"Stand back, give us some room!" one of the men said. Alan immediately recognised his voice. It was Scotch Bob from the College Hospital in London. He gave some emergency treatment to the unconscious man, they then loaded the man into the ambulance and drove away with their sirens blaring and light flashing. A large breakdown lorry arrived on the scene and quickly pulled the damaged lorry off the road, and the police quickly had the traffic moving again. Alan looked around he could see a black dog in the distance. He began to go towards it, but as he got nearer, the dog faded away.

"Lady, come back!" he shouted. He suddenly felt a jolt to his chest, then another, he heard somebody say "Try again!" and another jolt shot through his chest. All went still after that and everything went dark.

Professor Lansbury had been taken to the Trauma unit of the University College Hospital in London. He was declared dead on arrival. Thomas was the first to reveal the body covered by a cotton sheet.

"Oh my God, it's the Professor!" he screamed. Brian quickly ran over and joined him.

"Quick let's get him to the operating table," said Brian, "and see if we can get his heart started" They used the defibrillator and after 3 attempts the Professor's heart began to beat. They then X-rayed his body to see what other injuries he had. Thomas was the first to spot the damaged spinal cord at the top of the neck.

"My God, look at that" he said, pointing at the negative. "With an injury like that he could be completely paralyzed." They also noticed the Professor had a broken leg and hip, although there was no sign of any other injuries, which surprised Thomas.

"Let's put him through the brain scanner" said Brian, "just to be sure." Then as they looked at the pictures on the machine the full extent of his injuries became apparent. The Professor had severed his spinal cord high in the back of his neck. He also had a slight bleeding of the brain which seemed to have clotted and stopped.

"I don't think the Professor will survive this," said Thomas "and if he does he'll be paralysed from the neck down."

"If he comes out of the coma, then he could still have some quality of life" said Brian.

"You know the Professor," said Thomas "he will not like being hooked up to all the monitors." They made the Professor as comfortable as possible, and then left the ward.

"All we can do now is hope he recovers" said Brian.

The Professor was in a coma for two weeks before there was any sign of recovery. When Alan opened his eyes, he tried to move his arm, but felt no sensation at all. He could not feel any part of his body. It was dark apart from a small light he could see in the corner of his eye. He moved his head slightly and could just see a dimmed light on the wall. His vision seemed blurred.

Alan did still not know where he was, he tried to call for help but his mouth did not open. His brain began to think of strange things, he closed his eyes hoping the horror would go away. But when he opened them again he was still there. He knew he was lying down, but where was he? Suddenly a bright light shone in his eyes, and he heard someone say: "His pupils are dilating alright to the light, so he must be conscious." The bright light went out, and for a moment he could not see anything, then slowly his sight improved. A face came into focus about twelve inches away, then he realised it was Brian.

"Can you hear me Professor?" said Brian. Alan did the only thing he could do, he blinked.

"He can hear me" said Brian, "he blinked. Quick, let's connect him to the EEG machine and monitor the eye movements."

Over the next few days Brian and Thomas explained to the Professor what had happened to him, with the help of the computer monitor. It was slow progress and it seemed strange to Brian and Thomas that the Professor's life had come full circle. He had pioneered the machines to give severely brain damaged and paralyzed patients a better quality of life, now he too was connected to the very same machines.

Brian and Thomas kept communicating with the Professor whenever they could find the spare time. His wife Gillian was at his bedside most days, holding his hand and talking to him, but there was no response, only a blink now and then. On the fifth day of the accident Brian was talking to the Professor. The monitor was blank for some time then written across the screen appeared the words: "Why didn't you let me die?"

Brian was taken aback, and for a while he didn't know what to say. He looked the Professor square in the face and said "Because there is a chance that one day we may be able to repair the damage to your spinal cord."

Another message appeared on the monitor screen: "That could take years. I don't want to be stuck here like a vegetable. Give me some morphine."

Brian got up and left the room, he had to, he was overcome with emotion. He hated to see the man he had admired for all these years in a situation like this. He went to see Thomas and told him what the Professor had said.

"We will have to tell his wife and let her decide," said Thomas. Gillian was back at her husband's bedside when the two men came into the room. After they had explained what the Professor had wished for, Gillian burst into tears.

"But can't you do anything for him?" she cried. The two men looked at one another and shook their heads.

"Mrs Lansbury" said Brian "It's probably best to let your husband go, without the life support machines he could not survive, it's the kindest thing to do." Gillian finally agreed and watched as Brian injected the overdose of morphine into the Professor's arm. She then held her husband's hand, as he slowly closed his eyes for the last time.

The cause of death was stated as from internal injuries, but Brian and Thomas were satisfied they had done what their boss had wanted, and he was now with his beloved dog.

There was a massive funeral a week later, paid for by the London hospital. The Professor was buried in his local village churchyard. On his gravestone was written: Professor Alan Lansbury, a great man who spent his life trying to save others.

Lightning Source UK Ltd.
Milton Keynes UK
UKOW03f0412170414

230123UK00002B/176/P